A FOREIGN COUNTRY IS THE PAST

Fernando Sdrigotti

A FOREIGN COUNTRY IS THE PAST

Influx Press
London

Published by Influx Press
www.influxpress.com
@InfluxPress

Published by Influx Press, London, UK, 2025
© Fernando Sdrigotti, 2025

The right of Fernando Sdrigotti, to be identified as the author of this work has been asserted in accordance with section 77 of the Copyright, Designs and Patents Act 1988.

This book is in copyright. Subject to statutory exception and to provisions of relevant collective licensing agreements, no reproduction of any part may take place without the written permission of Influx Press.

This edition 2025
Printed and bound in the UK by Clays
Paperback ISBN: 9781914391569
Ebook ISBN: 9781914391576

Cover design: Flavio Mancini
Text design: Laura Jones-Rivera
Editor: Kit Caless
Proofreader: Trudi Suzanne-Shaw

This book is sold subject to the condition that it shall not, by way of trade or otherwise, be lent, re-sold, hired out, or otherwise circulated without the publisher's prior consent in any form of binding or cover other than that in which it is published and without a similar condition including this condition being imposed on the subsequent purchaser.

CONTENTS

Light Bugs	1
Sunstroke	9
A Different World	15
Cicadas	27
Every Time You Light a Cigarette with a Candle a Sailor Drowns	41
Pier	51
Dust Magnets	55
Owl	67
Colour Theory	81
A Sense of Impending Doom	99
Tiles, Traces of Former Rooms, Pipes	115
When Things Were Good	121
Saints	139
Love Is a Curable Disease	151
Ashes	169
About these stories	*179*
About the author	*181*

LIGHT BUGS

The telephone goes off while Grandma washes the dishes and Grandpa watches the telly. No one ever calls this late, except for Ana's mother, so they stare at each other without uttering a word and let the phone ring and ring, and it feels like it could ring itself off the hook. Eventually, Grandpa gets up, rests his cigarette on the ashtray, and walks to the telephone, Mumbling something. He lifts the receiver and says "yes" a couple of times, while the cigarette ashes dangle dangerously. He listens for a few seconds and then he says "heading there" and hangs up, so hard the ashes topple over. He comes back to the table, sits down, takes one final drag and crushes the butt with the others.

"Of course, it was that mad woman!" he says.

"You shouldn't have answered!" says Grandma, drying a pot.

"She'd just keep calling until we did…" he says.

"How many times this week?" asks Grandma.

"Three, four? I've lost count. Come on kid, let's go," Grandpa tells me.

"I think he better stay here with me," says Grandma.

"But I might need to send someone for help," he says.

"Then I'll go with you," she replies.

"No, you stay. Remember how upset she got when you came along the other night."

"Whatever," says Grandma.

Soon we are leaving the house.

Ana has no age; she always wears bright red lipstick and bathes in strong perfume. Ana's mother has an age — she must be over two hundred years old — but has no name. Neither Ana nor her mother go out much these days, but then no one goes out a lot this time of the year, because it's too hot to venture out.

Their house is much bigger than ours — it's the biggest house on the block. It's built on two levels and there's a short curved stairway that connects the front garden to the front door, some steps above, I don't know exactly how many. In the carpeted reception room, there's a vertical piano, wooden bookshelves crammed with old books and assorted ornaments, and a pair of large sofas facing one another under a glass chandelier. A couple of paintings hang from a wall, and they look like some of my school assignments but according to Grandpa they're art and worth a lot of money.

At the back, there's a massive overgrown garden infested with rats. On certain hot nights, they can be heard howling — impossible to say if they howl because they enjoy or hate the heat.

A FOREIGN COUNTRY IS THE PAST

Bugs everywhere, so many of them flickering around the streetlights. They crash into one another, like those dodgem cars they've got in the fair downtown. They hover mostly near the glow but occasionally hit you in the face, or get in your mouth. The bugs, that is — the dodgem cars don't float around but crash against other cars at ground level, and they certainly don't hit you in the face or get in your mouth. God forbid.

"Stop daydreaming and watch where you walk: the pavement is full of dog shit," warns Grandpa. He's always warning me about things — like not to walk with my hands in my pockets in case I fall, not to cross my eyes in case there's a draft and I stay cross-eyed, not to say anything about Mum and dad in school in case the other kids beat me up.

Before climbing Ana's front stairs, I stop for a second to check the soles of my shoes: both are clean.

Ana was very close with the local priest, Father Aldo. She'd go to the rectory or he'd come to pray at her house. Their prayers would start around five or six in the afternoon and go on until quite late. One hot evening a couple of months ago — and I remember it was hot because the rats in Ana's garden had been howling — Grandpa and I were hanging out outside when Father Aldo left her house. He doddered to the kerb and sat on a truck tyre that someone had dumped there earlier that day. He rested for a while, nodding off. Then he flipped the tyre upward with some effort, got it rolling in front of him, and walked in our direction.

"Good night," he said when he walked past.

"Good night, Father Aldo," I said; Grandpa nodded.

"Have a great evening," he added, stopping to send a sign of the cross towards us. Then he continued to follow the tyre down the road and disappeared round the corner. He seemed tired but in a good mood. And there was something saintly about him that night, glowing in the light and crowned by a halo of bugs.

"Why is he zigzagging like that?" I asked Grandpa.

"It must be the heat," Grandpa said.

"And why is he pushing that tyre?"

"That only God knows," said Grandpa.

A week later Father Aldo was dead. And then the calls started.

Five, six, seven, eight, nine steps. So there were nine steps to the front door, which is disappointing, because unlike ten, nine is a boring number. Grandpa opens the door with the spare key we keep at home. The lights are on but there's no one around — the paintings aren't on the wall any more either. He calls a few times to announce we're in, and soon Ana's mother appears, pushing her walking frame.

"Thanks for coming so quickly," she says.

"Where is she?" asks Grandpa.

"In the bathroom," Ana's mother says.

"Right... You stay here with her. I'll be a couple of minutes," says Grandpa before disappearing down the corridor.

"Come with me, boy," the old woman says and sets off towards the kitchen with surprising control of her walking frame.

A FOREIGN COUNTRY IS THE PAST

Soon I'm sitting at the table as she rummages in a cupboard. There's a pile of unwashed plates in the sink, the trash bin in the corner is overflowing, there are a million flies fluttering around the room, and the air stinks of naphthalene, because Ana's mother stinks of naphthalene. I guess it's only a matter of time until Grandpa and Grandma start stinking of naphthalene too, like all old people.

This thought makes my stomach hurt.

When the calls became regular, Grandma said that perhaps we should change our telephone number. She even went to the telephone company to speak with someone she knows there. But since it takes several years for new number requests to be processed, the plan was abandoned.

Ana's mother finds what she was looking for: a glass biscuit jar. She opens it with difficulty and then hands me one biscuit. Just one biscuit, placed in the middle of the table before me, no plate, no napkin — just the one biscuit.

"Go on, boy, have a biscuit," she says, and rolls out of the kitchen.

Now on my own (with the flies), attracted by its irresistible appeal, I bite the Mummified but soggy biscuit. It tastes like a dog turd that's been left out to dry in the sun but that was also caught by a drizzle — maybe this is the dog shit Grandpa warned me about earlier. I chew and swallow once and then toss the bitten biscuit on top of the trash in the bin. And I just sit there, swatting flies away, filling my mouth with saliva to wash away the stale taste.

A few minutes pass. When I'm sure that Ana's mother won't return, I leave the kitchen and head to the bathroom, which is at the end of the corridor, to the right.

Soon I'm facing a partially-closed door that fails to contain Ana's perfume. Grandpa is saying something on the other side but I can't make it out. I move closer to spy through the gap: Ana is sprawled face down on the floor, with her skirt rolled halfway up her back — there's a puddle under her, most likely perfume from all the bottles scattered all over the place. Grandpa, with his back turned to me, is trying to lift her. He pulls from her armpits but Ana makes no effort to help; she hasn't passed out and moves her legs, kicking the toilet bowl limply now and then, but it's as if her head were glued to the floor.

"Come on, woman!" says Grandpa. He pulls once more, then sighs and lets go, and Ana slumps once again.

He sits on the edge of the bathtub, takes his hand to his chest and gets his cigarettes out from the front pocket, taps the packet on his right knee a few times. Here he spots me. "Instead of standing there come and help me pull her up," he says, putting the cigarettes away without lighting any. I walk into the bathroom. "You grab this elbow and I'll grab the other and we'll pull at the same time... When I tell you..." he instructs. Here Ana realises there's someone else in the bathroom. She lifts her head and stares at me with foggy eyes — she attempts a smile.

"I'm sorry," she says.

"Hi Ana..." I say.

"OK pull!" says Grandpa and I pull, doing my best not to end up on the floor next to her. Ana starts to get up with our help and manages to get on her knees. Here she realises she's half-naked and yanks her skirt into place.

"I'm sorry," she repeats.

Eventually we get her on her feet. Grandpa, still holding her, tells me to go back to the kitchen. I leave them alone and rejoin the flies.

The clock on the wall now seems to move in slow motion and once it appears to me as if the arms were moving backwards. Some minutes or hours later (or earlier) the stench of naphthalene announces Ana's mother's return. She stands in the doorway and asks if the biscuit was good and I say it was. She nods several times, then sits and stares at me from behind her huge glasses — she doesn't say anything, just stares at me. I try to stare back but my eyes keep drifting away, chasing the flies around the room. Amidst the naphthalene stench, I can still smell the most penetrating notes of Ana's perfume.

At some point Grandpa joins us and says he's put Ana in bed. Ana's mother thanks him; she cries a few tears but not many. She offers Grandpa a cup of coffee but he declines. So she says she'll give us some biscuits, that I can eat them at home. Grandpa tells her that she shouldn't bother. She doesn't bother. We leave.

The calls will continue over summer but my Grandparents won't answer the phone any more; instead they'll unhook the handset and stick a pen in the dial for a couple of hours. Until the calls end for good come autumn, when Ana falls headfirst down the front stairs, who knows from which one of the nine steps. There will be a funeral that we won't attend, the house will get sold, the garden will get cleared, and the rats will escape to the neighbouring houses. And Ana's mother will end up in an old people's home by the river, living well into her two-hundred-twenty, subjecting her visitors to biscuits and the stench of naphthalene. And then Grandma and Grandpa will die too, within a couple of months of each other.

But none of this has happened yet.

Now it's still summer and we're back in the front garden. Grandpa smokes in silence, leaning against a tree, while I sit on the low front wall, looking around. There's lightning up above and a soft breeze that smells of wet grass. And the bugs are still crashing into one another under the streetlights. So many bugs: a cloud that half-blocks the glare and buzzes around my head. Bugs that try to get in my mouth, my ears, my eyes. But perhaps they aren't just crashing into one another — perhaps they're dancing. That's what I'd do if I were a bug. I'd dance under the streetlights. I'd dance until the rain comes. I'd dance until it stops.

And then I'd keep dancing.

SUNSTROKE

It's the second time this morning that the lifeguard and a group of tanned men and women walk past, clapping, parading a lost kid. This kid is also crying: his eyes are red and swollen — he must have been lost for a while, before someone spotted him and took him to the lifeguard hut. Suddenly, a pudgy woman in a black one-piece swimsuit rushes towards the group. The kid's face broadcasts happiness first, and then, after the man carrying him on his shoulders unloads him on the sand, panic. The woman — very likely his mother — grabs the kid by the right ear and pulls him away to the safety of their parasol, her shouts audible, her words carried away by the wind. And a few minutes later, they pack up and leave the beach, the mother walking two or three metres ahead, the kid dragging the closed parasol on the sand, sucking tears and snot.

Martín and his grandmother watch the whole affair unfold from their spot a couple of sandcastles away. It's like watching two very similar episodes of the same soap opera. And a very similar drama will eventually play out once more. And over and over.

Martín's grandmother left the sunscreen in the hotel and she insists they stay in the shade for a couple of hours after lunch. Martín sulks and plays with the sand: digging holes and letting the sand fall through his fingers. But when his grandmother falls asleep with a magazine covering her face, Martín scampers to the shore.

There are other kids there, on their own, not paying attention to one another. So Martín sits on the sand with his feet in the water and watches the waves come and go. They come and go, they come and go, pushing sand towards his crotch, and with this primeval rhythm, Martín loses all sense of time. When his grandmother comes to pull him by his ear back in the shade, it could be ten minutes or ten hours later.

On the way back from the beach, Martín can feel the skin on his shoulders tighten under the weight of his T-shirt. After walking for a while in the heat they stop at the bus terminal for food and cigarettes. The mural of the famous dead poet is there: she's heading into the sea, her back towards Martín and his grandmother, about to drown, always about to drown, forever getting in the sea that final time. Apparently, she drowned because she was sad about something, but Martín's grandmother can't remember what she was sad about. Poets get sad about many things, she says.

Then they eat, watching the news on the small black-and-white television in their room. Soldiers in camo with painted faces shout at the camera from behind a fence, once again, this year earlier than the year before. They have long guns and as usual, seem very angry. Suddenly one of them points the gun at the camera and everyone runs away. He doesn't shoot but here Martín's head starts to hurt. His grandmother turns the telly off. Sons of bitches, she says, this will never end. Martín asks what she means with this will never end. She says don't worry, one day you'll understand.

After dinner they go out for an ice cream downtown and they sit on the cathedral steps. There's a group of mimes here, surrounded by families — everybody is laughing hysterically. When the mimes start passing a hat around, everyone skedaddles. Martín and his grandmother walk away too, and into a store opposite the cathedral that's open until late — there's a small free seashell museum on its second floor. They go through the exhibition quickly, stopping only to admire a gigantic conch full of spikes. You could fit a whole person in it, Martín says. His grandmother says that conches don't eat people.

Then she takes him to the amusement arcade — three floors of flashing lights and shooting noises. She pays for ten tokens and Martín plays a game called Kung Fu Master and loses all sense of time. Ten minutes or ten hours later, they leave and stroll down the central pedestrian street, and then along the seaside promenade. In one of the souvenir shops there are three wax statues — one of them is a caveman with long black hair. His eyes are black and dead and his forehead is sweaty; Martín didn't know wax statues could sweat. The statue winks at him; Martín didn't know wax statues could wink. He throws up on the pavement

— orange and strawberry and little pieces of ice cream cone. His grandmother gets mad, says that she won't buy him another ice cream tonight. They go back to the hotel and straight to bed.

Martín dreams of winking wax statues and a giant camouflaged conch eating the famous poet, his Grandpa, his Mum and dad. It's always the camo, always the camo, as the conch turns into the angry soldier with a long gun, who comes running towards him. He wakes up screaming and his grandmother runs to his side and asks what happened. He can't say what happened; my head hurts, he says instead. She touches his forehead and pulls a serious face. And my shoulders hurt too, he adds. So she tells him to get up and remove the T-shirt: he has big swollen blisters on his shoulders. I told you to stay in the shade, I told you, she says, and then goes to the bathroom and runs a bath. Some minutes later, Martín is shaking in the cold water. When he goes back to bed, he has to lie face down because his back is covered in cream. He barely sleeps but he isn't fully awake either.

The next morning, his grandmother takes him to see Mr Kelly, the hotel manager, who's also a healer. He'll cure your sunstroke, she says, while Mr Kelly, Mumbling a prayer, places an enamel bowl on his head and then throws a piece of burning cotton inside. The cotton sizzles when it sinks in the water. He covers the burning cotton with a glass. And just like that, Mr Kelly cures Martín's sunstroke.

Martín's grandmother tries to shove two red banknotes in Mr Kelly's hand but he rejects them, saying he can't accept money, just light a candle to the Virgin when you go past the church. Of course I will, she says, and you say thank you; Martín says thank you. Then they go back to their room and get ready for the beach.

The sun is weak but Martín's grandmother says don't leave the parasol, you are already red like a shrimp; if he doesn't do what she says, she won't take him to the amusements tonight. Martín stays put, playing with a plastic straw, doodling in the sand.

And another group of tanned men and women walk by, clapping, parading another lost kid. But this kid isn't crying — he looks like he's having the time of his life on the lifeguard's shoulders. And as the men and women in swimming suits disappear behind the parasols, Martín wishes it was him they're clapping for. He wishes it was him who got lost. He wishes it was him they're carrying away. Where to? He doesn't know. He only knows he'd much rather be elsewhere.

A DIFFERENT WORLD

They arrive at the corner with the bank and the shops when they spot Elia rushing towards them, her backpack following a few milliseconds behind. When she reaches them, she stops and leans against a wall.

"You better go back!" she says, when she's managed enough air to speak.

"Go back where?" replies Sami.

"Home!"

"But why?" asks Muriel.

"Because school's off!" shouts Elia.

"Off?" asks Sami.

"I swear to God!" replies Elia. "Raids again!" she adds.

"Really?" asks Sami.

"I arrived early and they sent me back home. They said it was dangerous to stay."

"Will they raid the school? That doesn't make any sense…" says Muriel.

"You do whatever you want but I'm going home!" says Elia and dashes off. Sami and Muriel watch her run, until she reaches the corner and turns left and they can't see her any more.

"What shall we do?" asks Sami.

Muriel thinks for a couple of seconds, looks around and sees that the shops are all closed, there's no one around, no passing cars, the dogs aren't barking, no birds are up in the sky, the wind doesn't blow, there aren't even clouds.

"Let's go back home," she says.

Like the streets, the house is empty.

But all of this emptiness isn't unusual. It's December and it's already too hot to be outside this time of the day. Muriel's mother and father are at work and she should be at school — two different types of emptiness, both explained. So perhaps, since she's in the house — removing and dropping her backpack, kicking the shoes into a corner, then running towards the aircon and turning it on full blast — the house is busier than normal. That's the unusual thing.

She switches the telly on, and after a couple of seconds, there they are: the raids. Big red letters announce them, to a background of dramatic music. And in case someone could have possibly missed this from just staring at the screen, a presenter is talking about the raids, explaining that the same happened last year around this time, that it was the same the year before, and the year before the year before, that no one can remember life without raids any more. He says that it's all surely linked to the heat and the proximity of Christmas, pressure building. More than raids it sounds like a weather event — almost like one of those mad December storms that every single soul here both longs for and fears. But it isn't a weather event and last year the raids got quite scary, and the raiders — who came from past the train tracks — reached the boulevard. Canaves, the baker, climbed to the roof with a shotgun and said he'd shoot anyone who tried to break into his shop. He managed to keep the raiders out, made it into the local paper, and was praised as a hero by many in the neighbourhood, which was good for his business, judging from the new van he bought. But the raiders didn't disappear that day — instead they looted and burned the corner shop to the ground. There were rumours they also broke into some houses but it was all "someone's cousin has a friend who has a girlfriend who knows someone whose house got raided".

Here Muriel feels a pang of panic and sprints to the kitchen to get a knife from the worktop stand. Then she goes to the reception room and pushes the sofa against the door. After the sofa is safe in its new spot, she drags the cupboard towards the sofa, making sure the glass doors remain shut and that none of the Capodimonte figurines that used to belong to her Grandma falls off. Finally she pushes the armchair against the cupboard and sits down, clearing the sweat from her forehead with the back of the hand that's holding the knife. She waits. What she's waiting for, she doesn't know. She could be waiting for the raiders to break into the house. Or she could be waiting for her parents to return from work, in which case the barricade would be counterproductive. And if the raiders wanted to break into the house, couldn't they just use the garage entrance? And there's nothing she can use to build a barricade there, not even the car. She feels stupid and slowly rearranges all the furniture back in place. She heads back to the kitchen and replaces the knife in the stand.

There is a certain rhythm to the raids.

Every twenty or so minutes, the TV presenter aborts his circular monologue in the studio in order to go live to some neighbourhood. There, on the streets, an agitated reporter and a camera that shakes as the cameraman tries to capture the evolving action: the raiders gathering in front of a supermarket, the police cars blocking the entrance, the tension building, the chanting and shouting, and soon the rocks falling on windscreens, someone — a police officer — loudly giving the order to retreat to stop things from getting worse, the police cars hitting reverse and the officers stepping back, the raiders moving in and cracking open the metallic shutters as if they were opening a tin of sardines. Once the shutters are gone, it's a free for all. Here the presenter in the studio resumes his monologue, while the reporter on the ground grows agitated, shoved by raiders as they exit the unfortunate shop. The presenter in the studio tells the agitated reporter to look after himself, because that kind of statement always adds a dose of drama to the already dramatic scenes. And here the reporter and the cameraman cross to the other side of the road, from where they can get a better angle of the raiders leaving the supermarket with boxes and bags of food, but also crates of beer and wine. The sight of beer and wine vexes the presenter in the studio, because no one hungry would loot beer and wine, he says. The raiding and the commentary go on for another twenty minutes or so — until the shop is empty. Here the police reinforcements arrive and soon they start firing tear gas, then rubber bullets, and the raiders disperse, and the police — under a shower of stones — catch one or two of the slow raiders, generally old or disabled. The transmission ends as the crew struggles for air and they cut to the studio, where more monologuing takes place, and in twenty minutes or so everything kicks off again elsewhere. Occasionally the studio presenter will mention a death here or there, but death isn't something that matters unless you can actually see it. And this isn't the kind of thing they'd show this time of the day.

Muriel turns the telly off. But as she doesn't have anything else to do, she turns it back on. And then back off again. And then back on. There is a rhythm to this too.

Later she climbs the stairs to the top floor. She peers out from her parents' bedroom window without lifting the roller blinds. The street is still empty, but now it's almost twelve-thirty and everything is about to melt — she can actually see the heat lifting from the tarmac on the road below. Sirens and what sounds like a helicopter can be heard faint in the distance. Here the landline startles her and she runs out of her parents's room and down the stairs; she picks up the phone just in time — one always picks up the phone just in time.

"How are you doing?" asks Sami.

"I'm OK. Just a bit bored. No one's home."

"Same here. Have you seen the news? Raids everywhere…"

"It's the only thing they are showing…"

"It looks bad."

"Yes, it looks bad."

"Worse than last year. My aunt just called and said someone told her that they're already raiding past the train tracks."

"I can hear the sirens and a helicopter from here."

"You are *very* close to the train tracks."

"We aren't *that* close."

"Still…"

"You aren't that far either!"

"Well, I'm further than you! I can't hear anything from here. Still, it's scary!"

"Just stay in and throw the key on the door. It's not like they'll be raiding houses, right?"

"What about last year? They raided some houses last year, didn't they?" says Sami.

"Do you know anyone whose house got raided?"

"No, but I remember my aunt saying that a relative of someone from work got her house raided last year."

"People make up a lot of stuff."

"Who says what's to raid and what's not?"

"I think that they just want food. They are raiding supermarkets, not houses."

"It isn't only food! I just saw them taking crates of beer and wine! Didn't you see it on the news?"

"Do you have much beer and wine in your house, Sami?"

"No, I don't think so."

"Then you have nothing to worry about," says Muriel.

"What about the exam?" asks Sami.

"What's with the exam?"

"Do you think they'll postpone it until Monday or Tuesday?"

"No idea. I guess it depends on when the raids end."

"I really don't want to revise everything again and I don't think I'll be able to retain it all beyond Tuesday."

A FOREIGN COUNTRY IS THE PAST

"I'm sure you will remember everything."

"I just wish these raids wouldn't happen when we're supposed to be having exams. They should have them over the holidays!"

"It's the heat."

"And Christmas, I guess."

"Yes, that's what the guy on the telly said. Right, I've got to go now."

"What are you up to?"

"I thought I'd tidy up my wardrobe. Just to do something…"

"That's a great idea! I'll do the same."

"OK, speak later."

"Bye."

Seventeen knickers, twelve pairs of socks, six bras, nine T-shirts, and so on, not raided, but placed over her bed, arranged in different groups. Sorting the clothes takes Muriel about ten minutes. If it weren't so hot, she'd lie down in the sun and work on her suntan, so that when they go to the seaside in February, she isn't so white. But the last thing you want with these raids is heatstroke. And it would feel a bit immoral, lying in the sun, working on her suntan, while people are out there raiding shops. Not that she can do anything. But she definitely can watch the raids on the news. So she goes back to the kitchen, heats up the plate her mother left in the microwave oven, and turns on the television again. More of the same, only that the dead are now ten, which for some reason is a serious number. Perhaps to underscore the gravity of this number, there's now a small puddle of blood on the screen. And soon the puddle is joined by the customary red letters: TEN DEAD IN CLASHES BETWEEN RAIDERS AND THE POLICE. The blood puts her off the chicken escalope. She gets up and bins it. Here the telephone rings again.

"Yes?"

"Oh, I'm glad you are home!" says her mother.

"School was cancelled," says Muriel.

"I thought it might be. Don't you go out of the house! I'm back around six as usual but if you stay home, you'll be fine."

"Where would I go, Mum?"

"I don't know. But let's not find out today. Did you heat up the leftovers from last night."

"Yes. I've finished them already," she says and at the same time regrets binning the food, because she knows she'll get hungry again eventually.

"Good."

"What are we having for dinner tonight, Mum?"

"No idea but I didn't have a chance to do the shopping and now with the raids everything will be closed."

"It will..."

"But don't worry: I'll grab something on the way home. I don't know, a couple of pizzas..."

"I'm sure all the pizzerias will be closed too!"

"You are right... Well, I'll defrost something then. We'll figure it out."

"OK, Mum."

"Have to go now. Bye!"

"Bye, Mum," says Muriel but her mother has already hung up. She puts the phone down — it rings again immediately.

"Hey, it's me again," says Sami. "Couldn't get through!"

"I was on the phone with my Mum. What's up?"

"OK, so my aunt just called again. She says the army is already on the streets. One of her friends saw a truck full of soldiers speeding along the boulevard."

"Really?"

"That's what she said. Oh, and she said in the end there weren't raids earlier, past the train tracks, but it's definitely happening now… I guess it'll soon spill over to your side…"

"Did your aunt say that too?"

"Yes. And I've just seen it on the news."

Muriel stares at the television: they are showing images of raids in a neighbouring town.

"Where did you see it?"

"Channel 5," says Sami.

"Wait a minute." Muriel puts the phone down, walks to the telly, changes from Channel 3 to Channel 5. She recognises the gates of the football club where a couple of years ago, when she was still in the local primary school, she used to go for P.E. one afternoon a week. Crossing the tracks was an adventure then, even before the raids. She hasn't been that side of the tracks for a couple of years now, because it's too dangerous. There are people gathered outside of the club: mothers holding babies in their arms, young children, old people, the kind of people you see out and about every day; none of them particularly look like raiders — they just look like people from the other side of the tracks. She goes back to the phone, picks the receiver up. "You were right…"

"Told you! You never believe anything I say!"

"I do believe you! Your aunt not so much…"

"That's rude!" says Sami.

"What do they want there at the club?"

"The presenter said that they must be gathering there to go and raid the shops down the road. There's a supermarket there. A big one."

"It has to be that."

"Why don't the police do something?"

"No idea," says Muriel. "What could they do?"

"Arrest them? Shoot some of them?"

"Are your parents back home yet?" asks Muriel.

"No. They arrive around six. "Did you eat lunch already?"

"I just did," lies Muriel. "But I'm still hungry…"

"Do you think we should go out and raid a supermarket?" jokes Sami.

"I would kill for a pizza right now…" says Muriel.

"A pizza would be—" says Sami and the call ends.

Muriel tries calling Sami a few times but the line is engaged. Maybe the raiders broke into Sami's house. Or it could be a technical problem — like every summer when it gets so hot that cables melt, substations blow up, and the power or phone cuts out in part of the neighbourhood, sometimes all of it. On the other hand, wouldn't it be cool if Sami's house got raided? It'd bring the raids closer and yet keep them at a safe distance. But, of course, that's not what Muriel wishes would happen.

She puts the handset down, walks to the fridge, gets a couple of ice cubes from the freezer, fixes herself a large glass of Coca Cola, and comes back to sit in front of the TV. Not much seems to be happening outside the club. The raiders gathered there just hang out in the heat, talking to one another, while the camera pans over their sweaty faces and the presenter in the studio speculates if the army will finally disperse them or not, if the president will declare a curfew, when the raids will end, when things will ever go back to normal, because there was a time when raids weren't a thing, no matter how much we take them for granted now. Yes, it's hard to believe things were ever normal, he says. It's hard to believe all of this is going on.

Muriel takes a sip from her glass — it's so cold her teeth sting but the bubbles tingle her palate, so it's also a pleasant sensation. She doesn't recognise anyone on the telly, no matter how many times the camera fixes on a given face. She must walk past some of these people day in, day out, when they come this side of the tracks to do whatever they do over here. But it feels like a different world, a completely different world, she thinks, as the cold bubbles burst in her mouth one by one, and she sighs as if starring in a TV advert.

CICADAS

It's as if someone had turned their volume down or shut a window. Or as if they had thrown a massive towel over them, to silence them, because everything and everyone has to be quiet, that's what Auntie Clara said. No noise until five, and that includes the cicadas, because everyone always does what Auntie wants. Or else.

That's the first thing that comes to her mind after becoming aware of the sound of her body crashing against the surface, that sound that involves water but also air, as one element penetrates the other. After that initial sound — and the bubbly moments that followed — there was an eerie silence and now the cicadas aren't completely gone but they aren't completely there either, on the other side of the surface, singing. They are muffled and their otherwise piercing bickering is softened, the high ends blunted, like when the neighbour from the ground floor flat finally put a silencer on his motorbike exhaust, after months of everyone in the building complaining to the administrators. And the lower she sinks, the more the cicadas recede to the background, almost as if they were that same silenced motorbike driving away, or at least that's how it feels for the few seconds it takes her body to stop sinking — the time it takes her to reach the bottom. It's a brief sliver of time — a second, no more than that — but it stretches into eternity. Time stands still, as she holds her breath and her mind stalls, unable to grasp what's happening, latching onto the cicadas instead, as if she needed this right now, as if she no longer had a body to worry about.

And the thing with the cicadas is that you never think of them while they are there. You get used to the cicadas and you stop hearing them, just like you get used to everything else. Perhaps you just think a bit about them when the singing starts. Early summer first — here are the cicadas, they hadn't been around for a while. Then, for some days, you hear them around lunchtime, when they turn up for the afternoon shift. And after a while, you only notice them when they go quiet. At some point in the day they stop, always, almost all at once, more often than not when the sun comes down, or the storm arrives and the temperature drops, and now you notice that the cicadas aren't there any more and you remember they once existed. The next day they start singing again, eventually, but you don't think about them, because they are already part of the setting. And you stop hearing their absence too. Like this for months and the next thing you know, it's already too cold for the cicadas, autumn has arrived, and who the hell knows where they go, or whether they all die when the summer dies too, and the leaves begin to fall from the willow tree, and they mess the swimming pool, and Uncle Daniel gets mad and threatens to chop it down, but he never does, even if Auntie Clara would love it if the tree got felled. The cicadas are suddenly gone for good and the air feels empty without them, and that's how you realise they're gone. But then there are more pressing concerns, more important things to worry about, because you can't get in the pool, because it's full of leaves and the water is rotten, and it's too cold to do it anyway

These thoughts make her sad. For a millisecond, or even less, it saddens her that the cicadas might all die like this, and that the leaves will fall, and that the pool will be a mess that you can't use until next summer. And thinking of leaves, there's the willow tree up there: it's starting to turn yellow. Or perhaps it's the light of the sun that make the leaves appear yellow, since some seconds or an eternity ago, they were still green. But the willow tree looks taller from down here, and the other trees look taller too, even the small blackberry tree which is just a bit taller than she is, and it now seems miles away, like everything else. And then there's the sun: its yellow rays shooting into the depths, dancing with the movement of the water in the breeze. Sometimes the sun catches her eyes and the leaves, the trees, the surface — all of it — vanishes and all that's left is just that golden light. Then everything returns and the swaying willow, the surface, the light, and so many things going on, too many to take in at once. So her mind comes back to the cicadas — it always comes back to the cicadas. For some particular reason it keeps coming back to the cicadas. Perhaps to avoid thinking she's drowning.

But before all of this, there was the trip in the car and the old Pekingese dog. The dog's stench was as unbearable as the idea that his eyes might pop out if she stroked him too hard, as it happens to all Pekingese dogs. The dog was asleep and he woke up just as they drove past a billboard advertising a fire extinguisher company with a strange name — he always wakes up when they pass that billboard, that's what Auntie Clara told her. He even barked after they passed the billboard, and started making this strange sound with his snout — it sounded like his nose was blocked and he was choking but her Auntie said that's how the dog breathes, that's how all Pekingese dogs breathe. She still thought that he couldn't have long to live, not with that breathing noise.

After the trip in the car and the Pekingese dog with the strange breathing noise, there was Uncle Daniel parking and unloading all the shopping bags, and soon Auntie Clara unlocking the front door, saying that the house stunk of damp, and opening the windows to let the air in. And then Uncle Daniel appeared with a leaf net that looked like the kind of weapon you'd use to catch giant butterflies, and he fished leaves, a plastic bag, and a dead bird out of the pool, while he complained about the huge willow tree for the first time of the day. And then there was Uncle Daniel getting the grill ready, starting a fire, and salting the meat, all the time drinking straight from a bottle of beer, one of the large ones, that was sweating all over the floor, just like Uncle Daniel. Then it was the crackling of the charcoal, some sparks burning Uncle Daniel's right arm and his curse — I shit on God — and an apology to no one in particular, although perhaps it was directed at God. Then he scrubbed the grease off the grill with an old newspaper, and then there was the smell of burning charcoal, and a while later, the smell of burning meat, that she always loved because it reminded her of summer. Then Auntie Clara set the table in the shade under the willow. And soon they were eating.

This time, it was just the three of them. Her father stayed home — of course he would after what happened last time — and cousin Iñaki is now too old to come and just hang out with her, and maybe cycle for a while, or hunt frogs, or burn ants with the magnifying glass, like they used to do before he started secondary school and became unbearable. Unbearable like the Pekingese dog, standing next to her while she was trying to eat a piece of black pudding. Both — the dog and Iñaki — probably smelled equally rotten too.

"Did you bring a magazine, something to draw with, a puzzle, or anything to do?" asked Auntie Clara.

"No, I didn't," she replied.

"Well, there's that pile of mags in there," Auntie Clara said, pointing towards the little toilet by the swimming pool, referring to the old comics.

"OK."

"After lunch Uncle and I will take a nap and you need to find something to do. Something quiet and in the shade. Actually, why don't you go and lie down for a bit in the hammock at the back? It's nice and cool under the big trees, and you can make all the noise you want there." Here Uncle Daniel looked at Auntie Clara and smiled and Auntie Clara smiled back; he poured more wine in his glass and then in Auntie Clara's. "Just for a couple of hours. Until it's safe to be in the sun and we can go back in the pool."

"And don't go in the pool on your own," said Uncle Daniel.

"I can't swim," she replied.

"That's why," Uncle Daniel said.

"I won't go in the pool," she said.

"Then, in the evening, we can go for ice cream to the new parlour. They have a really good chocolate and mint flavour. If you behave and let us sleep and don't get all charred under the sun like the last time... I don't want to get on your father's—" said her Auntie and she didn't finish the phrase. "Just don't be in the sun."

Here's when she realised for the nth time that Auntie Clara looked just like her mother, that they were two drops of water. Same face, same eyebrows, same nose. Maybe the same genes as well, and here she thought about her Auntie dying too. She'd still come to the house to spend the weekends with Uncle Daniel, and she'd prepare the salad, set the table under the willow, and she'd drink wine, in time, not now because eleven year olds aren't supposed to drink wine. And no one would take naps any more — they'd be abolished. Of course she didn't want Auntie Clara to die. It was just a thought, the kind of nonsense that just pops into your head out of nowhere. She knew it was just a stray thought but she still felt guilty about it.

"I will lie in the hammock and read some comics. Don't worry, Auntie," she said, to make the thought go away, to feel better.

Then there were the magazines.

She didn't go to the hammock but stayed under the willow, with the Pekingese dog who was also following Auntie Clara's directives and was napping under the table. Staying there instead of going to the hammock like she'd promised felt like a transgression — not a huge one, but just enough to feel like a small act of rebellion against the tyranny of the nap. Like necking the bottom of the two wine glasses that were left on the table, and after them, the bottom of the bottle. Wine tastes odd — how can anyone be into this kind of thing?

Nippur of Lagash was the name of the comic she had grabbed without thinking much. Some kind of warrior doing warrior things — all very violent, the kind of stuff her cousin and Uncle Daniel like to read when they are over here. The magazine was totally devoid of colour and the pages were all crumpled and stained with indeterminate substances. She read a couple of pages, and on the vignette where Nippur of Lagash sticks a knife into a crooked old man's right eye, she gave up. It wasn't that it was too gory but that it was silly boy stuff. And here, for the first time this summer, she noticed the cicadas. She noticed them, despite the faint dizziness from the wine.

They sing louder when people are taking a nap, was the first thing that crossed her mind. Then she wondered how on earth they make that racket. It had to be millions of them. Also, she had only ever seen dead cicadas. Were they ever alive? And this is how she started to climb the willow. She placed a chair by the trunk and then it wasn't that hard to clamber up. If the cicadas were ever alive, she'd be able to find one up on the tree. Not one — she'd find millions of them.

The last time her cousin was here, they fought over the hammock.

He wanted the hammock and she wanted it too. They

had an argument and he started to wind her up and she bought the fight. In the end she cried and her cousin laughed, said that if she wanted the hammock that badly she could have it. She said she didn't want it any more. He said he didn't want it any more either. Somehow they ended up cycling.

The sun punched hard on the cracked dirt road. Her cousin said that if she couldn't handle cycling under the midday sun, they could go back and wait until it got cooler. She said that she could handle cycling under the sun, no problem at all, that she didn't need to go back, unless he needed a break. Here her cousin laughed and darted away, until he disappeared after a bend. She kept pedalling, even though now she really did want to go back and leave him to his nonsense. But there was no way she was going to stop. And sure enough, after she got to the bend, there he was, waiting for her, pretending to smoke a cigarette whilst leaning against a tree. She kept pedalling, as fast as she could, and he jumped on his bike and caught up with her eventually.

A few minutes later, they arrived at the cemetery. Her cousin said he wanted to show her a new tomb, and asked if she was afraid of cemeteries. Then he said, "Of course you aren't," and she didn't feel the need to add anything to that, because she knew exactly what he meant. They left the bikes by the entrance and walked along the plots. All those tombs on the ground, with their old photos and dried flowers always made her sad, but nowhere near as sad as the niches on the wall. She didn't take in any of the faces — they all looked like the same black and white person. Suddenly her cousin stopped walking.

"This one," he said and pointed at the tomb before them.

It was the tomb of a young girl called Helga, possibly just a couple of years older than them in the photo.

"Who's that?" she asked.

"Her name was Helga."

"I can see that, fool. But who is she?"

"Was."

"Who was she?"

"A girl from town. Died earlier this year."

"I can see that too. And how did she die?"

"That's the interesting bit," said her cousin and sat down on the tomb.

"Tell me," she said.

"Right... so she was in the pool with some friends... Not far from our house... One of the big houses next to the social club... Do you know the club with the tennis courts on the way to the water tower?"

"I know the club, yes. And did you know her in person?"

"I saw her cycle past a couple of times, but I never spoke to her."

"She looked pretty."

"I think so, yes. Can't remember now, but I think she did."

"Well, she looks pretty in the photo at least."

"Everyone looks pretty in photos."

"No, not everyone."

"Girls do."

"And what happened?"

"You interrupted me... I was about to tell you. What happened is—"

"I won't interrupt you again."

"You did it again... Don't do it any more or I'll stop!"

he said and pressed her lips shut. "So… She was in the pool with some friends… It was during a birthday party… And she came out and went to change the cassette tape… Barefoot and wet, of course… And she got electrocuted and died: the end."

"Wow! That's sad."

"Yes. Sad, right?"

"Very sad! And how do you know all of this?"

"Dad told me. Everyone in town knows about it. Nothing ever happens here, no one ever dies, until someone does die, and everyone talks about them over and over."

"Like you are doing now."

"Exactly."

"Anyone else died?"

"Only old people. And those boys who crashed their car on the highway… They were coming from a disco…"

"When did that happen?"

"I don't know."

"How old were they?"

"I don't know that either."

"You are very bad at this," she said and they both laughed and he pushed her and she stumbled but didn't fall.

Then they wandered among the plots for a bit longer. And then they cycled back to the house. When they arrived, Uncle Daniel and Auntie Clara were still in their bedroom, so they stayed under the willow tree, pretending to read comics. But she couldn't stop thinking about Helga. Her name was unusual — she didn't know that kind of name existed. Maybe that's why she died, she thought, knowing very well it was a terrible explanation.

A FOREIGN COUNTRY IS THE PAST

When Auntie and Uncle woke up from their nap, she was already starting to feel lightheaded. That night, back at home, she vomited after dinner and her dad had to drive her to A&E. It was an overreaction, of course. It was just sunstroke, nothing out of the ordinary. But her father was overreacting a lot since her mother had died seven months earlier. There was no point in getting into an argument with him about any of this. He, on the other hand, got into an argument with Auntie Clara and Uncle Daniel, about how she'd got all burnt cycling under the midday sun. He threatened not to let them see her any more; he didn't say it to their faces, but was moaning about it for a few days. And then somehow she found herself spending most weekends with them again. The woman who kept calling at night might have had something to do with it, because her father was suddenly in a much better mood, dressing in his good clothes, and shaving every day again.

Her grandfather had planted the willow when her mother was born. If he had planted a tree for Auntie Clara she didn't know. Perhaps he hadn't, because Auntie Clara hated it. But she liked the idea that the tree was for her mother and that her Auntie hated it — it felt fitting that this was the place to start searching for living cicadas. Such a lovely willow - it looked almost like a hairdo. And such a strong tree — the thicker branch extended over the pool, halfway in. She felt safe sitting on it, searching for the source of the cicadas' sound.

Their song was definitely louder up here but still she couldn't see any, no matter how close she looked. She kept moving slowly, dragging herself along the branch, and suddenly the idea hit her: it wasn't the cicadas that were making the noise but the trees. Of course it was the trees! That's why she had never seen a living cicada. And where did the dead cicadas come from? Because she had seen dead ones more than once. That, she didn't know yet — there was time to figure it out later. For now that she knew that the trees were the source of the sound, she could even feel the willow shifting beneath her. It was alive, really alive. Alive, and surrendering to her weight. Just enough to make her stumble and fall into the pool.

And here there was the splash.

And now there's just the shimmering water and the sun in her eyes and the sound of the muffled cicadas. Or the muffled trees, because it's the trees that sing — she hasn't forgotten this, not even with the shock of suddenly finding herself pressed against the bottom of the pool. And now there's the muffled barks and the dog's ugly face staring at her from above, while he barks like mad, with his Pekingese eyes still in their sockets.

Soon the water stops dancing and another body breaks the surface and rushes towards her, all full of bubbles and hair. She inhales and water fills her lungs, and then Uncle Daniel's strong arms wrap around her and lift her to the surface in one move.

The next thing the singing trees and the barking dogs are no longer muffled and here's the air, and the chills, and the coughing, and the water leaving her lungs through her nose and mouth, and then leaving her eyes too — everything happening at once.

A FOREIGN COUNTRY IS THE PAST

Uncle Daniel asks if she's OK and she nods to say she is, in-between coughs and sobs. She attempts to get some air in, and this makes her sound like the Pekingese dog. Uncle Daniel hugs her and she cries on his shoulder and she could cry herself to sleep.

"You could have drowned!" he says and she cries even more. "Thank God I heard the dog bark!" he says and he rubs her head while she can't stop crying, might never be able to stop.

And she can't say anything either. She can't tell him about the cicadas, or the willow, or how it's the trees that sing. She can't tell him about the bike ride to the cemetery, or Helga, or her mother. She can't tell him anything. She can just cry and hope that the moment when Auntie Clara arrives is delayed forever. Or that at least when she arrives, the tears have stopped flowing. At least that. Since tonight there won't be any ice cream. And the summer will soon be over.

EVERY TIME YOU LIGHT A CIGARETTE WITH A CANDLE A SAILOR DROWNS

Moustache pulled up at noon in his metallic brown Dodge 1500. An ugly car with an ugly colour. It looks like a potato — a likeness heightened by how infrequently he visits the carwash. And he loves a Dodge 1500 — he must've had three of them already. I don't get it. Peugeots, Renaults, Fiats, Jeeps, Chevys, Valiants, Fords, even Citröens are better. So many cars to choose from and he goes for the ugliest of them all. Of course the main reason why I don't like the car is that it's *his* Dodge 1500.

I was determined to have a bad day, like every Saturday we spend together. It didn't matter that visiting a cargo ship was definitely an upgrade from going to Unclc's bar for a Coke and a ham and cheese toastie (which Moustache never pays for — a detail Mum keeps bringing up), visiting some distant relative, or ending up in the nurse's office in the clinic, playing darts with a polystyrene board and used surgical needles, because he's had some last minute emergency, very likely with one of the nurses (something Mum can't stop bringing up either). All of these non-activities suck, so last year, as I was getting out of his car after one of our Saturday rollercoasters, I said I didn't want to see him the following week because I get bored to death when he takes me out, and I'd much rather stay home watching the telly or playing with the dog. Here an argument ensued and he said that Mum is brainwashing me into hating him, and I replied that if he was concerned with my upbringing maybe he shouldn't have left when I was just one. He smacked me. I sucked up my tears and hurried into the house without giving him the pleasure of crying in front of him. And I didn't cry in front of Mum either.

After this, I refused to meet him for three months, giving no reasons to Mum, not that she ever asked why Moustache wasn't coming any more. Then he bought the Atari console for Christmas and I still didn't want to see him, but I wanted the Atari console, so I extended an olive branch, and he started calling once a week again, to pretend to be interested with how I was doing in school, for thirty seconds to a minute at a time, which wasn't that much to ask of me, considering the Atari.

And then as the ship was reaching the city, the Hungarian captain's wife got ill, and that's how she ended up in Moustache's clinic. Then the Hungarian captain invited Moustache to visit the ship. And the following Saturday Moustache was ringing the bell, at the usual time. His usual car, dirty as always, was waiting outside. Waiting like only a potato can wait.

A FOREIGN COUNTRY IS THE PAST

We were both quiet during the trip. He didn't apologise for the smack, and I didn't ask for an apology either, because I understood the Atari console was his way of saying sorry. The windscreen wipers, on the other hand, were very loud and busy throwing water to the sides; first through the suburbs with their sad low houses, then across the city centre with all those ugly skyscrapers, and then while Moustache was parking in a quiet corner of the dock, watched over by cranes and old warehouses, leftovers from when this was a busy port rather than a mere waypoint for ships heading to the capital. He repeated a few times that parking in the rain was tricky, especially since the direction of the potato could do with a service, but somehow he managed to park. Then, after lighting a cigarette with the car's lighter, he rubbed the windscreen with his left hand, opened his window slightly to let the smoke out, and nodded towards the only visible ship.

"That's the one," he said, as if I could have possibly missed it.

"Which one?" I asked, just to be difficult.

"That one. There's only one ship there... The one with the Panama flag," he added.

"But you said the ship was from Hungary," I protested, now genuinely confused.

"It is. But she sails under a Panama flag," he answered, and I had no idea what that meant.

We left the car and ran towards the ship in the rain, covering our heads with our windbreakers. There was a long boarding ramp connecting the pier to the deck, which was floating a few metres above. We walked slowly up the steps, Moustache showing amazing skill at keeping his cigarette dry in the rain. At the top of the ramp we were met by two armed sailors, both dressed in their funny sailor costumes. They greeted Moustache and he said that we were coming to see Captain Something, who would meet us on the deck at one p.m. While I was studying their machine guns, one of them checked the papers on his clipboard and then asked Moustache for his ID. Moustache showed him his driving licence and then said that I was with him, that he didn't have an ID for me, but that I was only a minor delinquent, nothing to worry about. The sailors chuckled and waved us through and soon we were standing on the deck, sheltering from the rain beneath a rescue boat that was covered with a white canvas.

Five minutes must have passed and the deserted harbour became a boring sight. I said that maybe we should leave and Moustache answered we would wait, because he wanted me to see a real ship. I said that even sponging a Coke and a ham and cheese toastie off Uncle was better than standing in the rain. Moustache's face tensed and I anticipated a smack. In the end, he didn't hit me. He just lit another cigarette and continued to smoke in silence.

A couple of minutes later, I'm following Moustache and the Hungarian captain through a dark corridor. I can hear the Hungarian captain speak in broken Spanish but I can't make out exactly what he says. And I can't understand why a Hungarian would have darker hair than us — I imagined he'd be violently blond. And why is he dressed in normal clothes? So many questions. Moustache turns around and tells me that we're going to see the engine room first, then the bridge, which sounds exciting as I've never seen anything like that before, but I don't want to let my excitement show, so I just nod.

We reach a flight of stairs and descend. Soon the Hungarian captain opens a door and we are slapped by a hot breeze and deafening mechanical sounds. He shouts that this is the engine room and waves us in. Inside, gigantic moving cogs and pulleys are everywhere, but there's no human being in sight. The Hungarian captain tries to explain something but soon realises that it's pointless with all this noise and makes a gesture, rolling his fingers in the air in a forward motion — the international sign for "later I'll tell you what this is all about". We walk across an elevated platform to the other side, cursed by steaming pipes, pumps, and who knows what's the name of all those other things, until we leave through another door, which leads to yet more stairs. The Hungarian captain shuts the engine room door behind us and the noise recedes. He mentions how many people work down there when the ship is sailing but I miss the number. Then, suddenly, we're climbing again and I struggle to keep pace.

A few more turns and we're on the bridge. Here, three middle-aged men dressed in naval uniforms square up and give the Hungarian captain a military salute. The Hungarian captain returns the greeting and everyone goes on with their business. This is a massive room with windows all around, more like a control tower in an airport than something you'd expect to find in a ship. Through the windows I can see the river and the delta disappearing into the distance. There are screens and levers everywhere, but the ship's wheel is nowhere to be seen. Moustache must have intercepted my thoughts, because I hear him ask the Hungarian captain about the wheel. The captain says that there isn't a wheel as such in this kind of ship any more, and then he walks to one of the computers and points at a device that looks like one of my Atari joysticks. He jerks it and says "this is the wheel now!" and laughs. Then he says that I can have a go if I want. So I move closer to the joystick and start pressing buttons and the ship makes a loud noise and suddenly we're sailing away downstream, until the river meets the ocean, and then we're out battling huge waves, and thank God I'm a good captain, because otherwise we'd sink like the Titanic, and I'm doing quite well, until suddenly we bump into a whale, and the ship stops, and we're all thrown forward, like when a bus suddenly breaks and all the passengers end up stacked towards the front. The Hungarian captain laughs — Moustache looks stressed. Soon I get tired of all this naval mischief and let go of the joystick and we're back in the port.

"Good, isn't it?" says the Hungarian captain.

"Yes. That was fun," I say. Moustache looks relieved. I'm not sure if it's because he gets seasick, or because he was afraid I'd break something and that he'd have to pay for it.

The Hungarian captain shows us around the bridge a bit longer and then we proceed to his cabin. Naturally, there are more stairs and hallways. That's my main takeaway about ships: they are filled with stairs and hallways.

And here, in the Hungarian captain's cabin, we meet the Hungarian captain's wife. I have never seen a woman this blonde and tall before, except in films, and this is exactly how I'd imagined Hungarians would be. And she doesn't look like someone who was recently ill. She smiles and moves her head a lot when the Hungarian captain introduces her. I don't catch her name but it starts with an A.

The Hungarian captain explains that his wife doesn't speak Spanish or English, only Hungarian. She smiles once more and then apologises (I suppose) in her language, and heads to a small kitchen area at the other end of the cabin. The Hungarian captain invites us to sit around a small table, by a tiny window — everything is small in his cabin, except for the woman whose name starts with an A. I sit against the wall, with my back to the river. I watch her handle a coffee pot, cups, and some biscuits. She must be two and a half metres tall and her head almost touches the ceiling; but she's slim and her movements are very precise. She lifts the biscuits with her long, thin fingers and slowly places them on a plate; her hands look like a stork, or some other delicate bird, and I don't like birds but I like her fingers — I like them a lot. And I think that soon I will be taking those biscuits to my mouth and I have this strange feeling in my stomach, as if I had swallowed a woodlouse. Here she turns around and says something in Hungarian and shakes me out of my daydream.

"She asks if orange juice is OK for the kid," says the Hungarian captain.

"Yes, that will be OK. Anything for the kid," Moustache says. The word "kid" makes my ears ring as much as Moustache's slap in the metallic brown Dodge 1500 some months ago. She smiles at me and I smile back at her and she turns around to go back to her chores.

The conversation between Moustache and the Hungarian captain switches to English. The only thing I can recognise as a word, here and there, is "people", which sounds to me like the name of a famous TV clown called "Pipo the Fisherman". But I have no idea of what this means, or whether they are indeed talking about Pipo the Fisherman, which would make some sense, since the Hungarian captain is a man of the sea. Meanwhile, the smell of coffee spreads through the small cabin. The Hungarian captain's wife pours the coffee from the cafetière into a jug, fills a glass with orange juice from a carton, and then places everything on a tray and walks towards us. The way she carries the tray, the way she floats towards us, remind me of an air hostess — I've never been on a plane but I've seen them in films.

"She looks like an air hostess," I think aloud.

"Shhhh," says Moustache, grabbing me from the elbow and pressing. It hurts.

"Well, she's got the height to be one," says the Hungarian captain in his accented Spanish, smiling and proud. Moustache presses harder and I let go a quiet shriek — just enough for the Hungarian captain to notice what I'm being subjected to, but not his wife, who's now placing the food and drinks on the low table. "Oh, no! No need for that!" says the Hungarian captain. "He's a very clever kid!" Moustache lets go off my elbow. The captain laughs, Moustache laughs, the air hostess laughs too — they all laugh nervously. At some point, I start laughing too, though actually what I want to do is cry. But it isn't Moustache pressing my elbow that makes me want to cry. I don't know what I want to cry about.

Eventually we leave. By the time we've reached the potato, I've forgotten the Hungarian woman's face, but her fingers stay with me a bit longer.

A FOREIGN COUNTRY IS THE PAST

Moustache drives in silence, tapping his fingers against the wheel. He hasn't said anything about the ship, or the Hungarian captain, or the air hostess. He hasn't said anything about me taking the ship to the middle of the ocean and bumping into a whale. He hasn't said anything about his latest episode of parental violence. I want to say that the air hostess didn't look ill and ask what her problem was, but I feel Moustache will tell me I'm too young to understand, and I've had enough of that already. So I remain quiet, listening to the windscreen wipers spit water to the sides.

When we stop at some traffic lights downtown, Moustache opens the glove compartment and gets a new pack of cigarettes out. He presses the car lighter, removes the pack's ribbon and plastic, and soon the lighter pops out, smelling of burnt plastic. He lights his cigarette, takes a few drags, releases smoke through his nostrils. Then he lowers the window, enough for air to get in and water to stay out.

"Did you know that sailors believe that every time you light a cigarette with a candle, one of them drowns?" he says, out of nowhere.

"No," I answer.

"Apparently so."

"Why would I know that?"

"You kids know everything these days," he says.

"You should have talked to the captain about it," I reply.

"Yes, I should have," he says.

The lights change, the potato starts. Moustache drives in silence through the city centre and then through the suburbs. Twenty minutes and no more words later, he pulls up at home. The lights are on in the front room but the curtains are drawn. He opens the car door for me and nods. I say "Bye dad" as I step out. I rush to the house, covering my head with my windbreaker, keeping an imaginary cigarette dry, and ring the bell. The dog barks, lightning cuts across the sky, and then along comes the roar of thunder.

When Mum opens the door, Moustache has already disappeared down the road.

PIER

It's four-thirty but the sun still stings — it must be forty and it's so humid you could drown. We drag our feet on the burning pavement and try to shelter under the trees, but they aren't old enough to give shade; eventually we stop zigzagging and just walk in a straight line. The cicadas and the aircons blast their siesta muzak. A dog crosses the road and a car rushes past. The river is finally there, past the waterfront avenue.

Out of habit, we take the footbridge that lands on the pier. The pavement is tiled in mock-Copacabana style and the design, with its slopes and missing tiles, intensifies the brain fry. We pause for a bit in the middle, spit at the empty road below, and watch the old power station in the distance. When we get to the other side, we jump the railings and climb down to the beach.

The river is low this summer but there isn't much of a beach anyway — just a couple of metres of sand, some rocks, and plenty of junk. Opposite there's the yacht club's marina. There are people moving about on the boats, doing their boat people thing, perhaps getting ready to head out to the delta to catch the dusk, to get some fresh air, open a bottle of sparkling wine, have a great time getting eaten alive by mosquitos. We didn't come to see the boat people, so we keep walking along the pier, until we reach the stretch that opens out to the river. We spot Darío fishing in the distance, where the pier ends like a stump.

He's wearing the usual sleeveless vest, football shorts, flip-flops and a cap; he's drinking Tetra Pak wine, holding a fishing line with his left hand. Lucio whistles and Darío turns around — he seems happy to see us. When we reach him, he rests the wine on the sand and we shake hands. Then Lucio and I sit in the shade, under the pier. My right hand now stinks of fish.

I never understood fishing. The kind of thing they catch around here tastes like mud and petrol and fat. I think Lucio doesn't care about fishing either — I've never heard him mention fishing and I don't think he owns a fishing rod. But we need to kill time somehow, and the air feels better here — the air can be felt. Darío, on the other hand, can't get enough fishing. Ever since he got fired from his job at the garage you can pretty much guarantee he'll be here or at his girlfriend's. Since they broke up a month or so ago he might even sleep here.

Almost as if he were reading my mind, "Look," he says. He lifts his T-shirt — there are bite marks on his left flank.

"What happened?" asks Lucio.

"I went to get my bike from Rosa's and she released the dog on me," he says.

"Shit," says Lucio.

"And look," he says and lifts the right leg of his shorts — more bites.

"Jesus... What kind of dog does she have?" I ask.

"A German shepherd. But it was Rosa who bit me here!"

"Nah..." Lucio says.

"Yes, man, she fucking bit me!" he says and Lucio and I burst into laughter. At this exact moment Darío's left arm jerks. He pulls from the line and "Fucking hell," he says, drops the wine on the sand, grabs a piece of wood from the floor, and rolls the line around it; like this he starts to pull again. "It'll snap it!" he says. "The fucker will snap the line!"

"That must be huge!" says Lucio, now actually interested in fishing; he gets up and walks to the shore.

Darío pulls, releases, pulls again, releases again, pulls again — the routine goes on for a minute or so. The line looks like it'll break but it doesn't, and soon we can see the back of a turtle glimmering under the water. When the shape is about a metre and a half from the shore, Darío passes the line to Lucio, tells him to pull from the wood and not the line or he'll lose a finger, and heads to my right, to get a big slab of concrete that's fallen off the pier. He struggles to lift it but somehow manages, then runs back to the water and hurls it to where the turtle's head should be. Suddenly the line goes slack. Darío takes it from Lucio's hand and pulls the turtle to the shore — the water turns red around it but the river carries the blood away.

"Son of a bitch," says Darío, "it almost snapped it." The turtle wobbles its head in circles, like one of those dummies taxi drivers keep at the back of the cab. Lucio counts his fingers to make sure they're all there. Darío gets a hammer from his fishing bag, bends on his knees, and smashes it on the turtle's head several times, until it stops moving. All stillness except for a bubble of blood forming in the right nostril — in and out, until it bursts.

"Piece of shit, almost cut the line," says Darío while he removes the hook from the turtle's mouth, "I'll use it as bait. Help me crack it open," he says to Lucio.

"Do you really need to do that?" I ask.

Darío thinks for a couple of seconds, holding my stare in silence.

"You're right. I don't," he says, turns around, and nudges the turtle back into the water with his right foot. It sinks slowly until it disappears.

Lucio comes back to sit in the shade. In silence, we watch Darío bait the hook with chunks of meat. Soon he casts the line into the river. Before he catches anything else, we're gone.

DUST MAGNETS

"This is Nazi music," says Diego, taking a short break from rolling a spliff.

"You've already said that!" answers Beli.

"The record is skipping," says Ro, and he could be referring to Diego repeating the Nazi music jibe, or to the record now spinning on the turntable, playing the same four or five bars for the fourth or fifth time in a row.

"Yes, I've said it and I'm saying it again because this is Nazi music and we're still listening to it. And we're listening to the same bit over and over!" answers Diego. Beli jumps up from the corner of the sofa where he's sunk, sighs, and pushes the stop button — the music slurs into the low zones. "Thank you very much!" says Diego.

"You're welcome," says Beli. "And I'd rather not listen to you repeat the same thing over and over either. Is there any button I can press?"

"You can press here," says Diego, holding his crotch.

"Why do you say it's Nazi music?" asks Ro.

"Because the Nazis liked this guy," answers Diego.

"The Nazis liked many things," answers Beli. "They liked dogs, for example. That doesn't make dogs Nazis."

"Maybe dogs aren't Nazis, not all dogs at least, but

Wagner definitely is Nazi music," says Diego.

"You don't make any sense," says Beli.

"OK, well, whatever. Nazi or not, why can't you play something else? It's Friday and I'm bored to death," says Diego.

"I can't play anything else because this is the only vinyl I've got," says Beli.

"Then put a CD on. Or the radio!" says Diego.

"I wanted to show you the turntable!" says Beli.

"Can't you see we aren't interested?" says Diego.

"I was enjoying the EQ lights," says Ro, who's the most stoned of the three.

"Then just play that Nazi music but leave the volume down," says Diego and laughs.

"That's a good idea," says Beli, laughing too. He lowers the volume and presses play and the vinyl starts spinning again. Ro once more gets lost in the EQ lights. The lights move up and down — it's as if they were dancing just for him.

Beli caught the turntable from the corner of his right eye when he was walking past a pile of garbage; it was resting on top of some magazines and newspapers. Here no one ever throws anything away, he thought — it must be broken. He still carried it back home, along with a three LP set of Wagner's *The Flying Dutchman*. If it was broken, he'd just leave it outside again, and someone would find a use for it.

He plugged it into the hi-fi and to his surprise, the unbranded turntable worked. And the records, if quite scratched and skipping here and there, were still playable. Music sounded different through it; that is, music sounded different from music on cassettes and CDs. For one thing, there was the sound of the needle travelling in the groove, which you could hear — faintly — even if the volume knob was down all the way to zero. But the music sounded warmer too, even with a bit of hissing and scratching in the background. And that's all he could say about what it sounded like, because he wasn't into classical music, and had little idea of what to expect. But he was certainly into gadgets and this was a new gadget. And it was free.

He had never owned a turntable before. Boys his age rarely did, now that CDs were all the rage. Also national labels didn't press vinyl any more, so you were stuck with vintage or imported stuff, and that could cost an eye and a half. Of course, he would've had vinyl records at home if his mother hadn't tossed away a collection of one hundred — with the turntable — when his father died. Beli was too young to care about gadgets then, and when he later asked his mother why she had got rid of all that stuff, she said it was because the records were dust magnets and took up too much space in the lounge.

He wondered what music his father listened to. He couldn't remember ever seeing him put a record on. He could only remember him listening to the radio in the car. He certainly didn't come across as the kind of person who'd worry too much about music. What he was always worried about was his business, and he was right to be concerned, because it was his business that would eventually kill him. If he'd ever really been into music enough to amass a collection of one hundred LPs, then that must have been in a previous life. One before he was dead, but also one before he was half-alive.

Now they are out, walking in the evening heat. It's muggy and there are heavy clouds gathering above — at some point it'll rain and it might never stop, like it usually happens this time of the year. Ro starts singing the refrain from the overture of *The Flying Dutchman*.

"Nazi music!" says Diego, laughing.

"Oh, for fuck's sake!" says Beli. "Don't give him any more ammo, please!"

"Sorry, I can't stop singing it!" Ro answers and keeps humming the refrain. The other two tut to protest, for different reasons.

They're heading to a party a few blocks away from Beli's house. Some hipsters who squat an old abandoned house have been throwing parties every weekend, all through the summer. The squat is in a very central block, near the commercial district, in an area full of empty shops and abandoned offices — few (if any) can be bothered by the noise from the parties. There's always live music, and sometimes they screen European or Japanese avant-garde films — occasionally a porn flick too. There's even a bar and cheap cold beer — a crucial detail in a weather like this.

"It's getting annoying," says Diego.

"He's right," says Beli.

"Sorry, I can't stop!" says Ro. "I can't stop singing this Nazi stuff!" he says.

"I'm not getting in there with you unless you stop singing!" says Diego.

"Don't be so dramatic!" answers Ro.

"I'm not dramatic. I just don't like Nazis," says Diego.

"Oh, for fuck's sake, just stop with that!" says Beli.

Ro keeps singing, now in a higher octave.

A FOREIGN COUNTRY IS THE PAST

Some bars later they arrive at their destination. There's a line of kids waiting to get in. The air smells of weed and there are some familiar faces, but no one greets anyone because that's the thing to do these days.

They wait and eventually someone opens the door and lets everyone in.

The vinyl spinning, the needle struggling to stay in the groove, shaking in its magnetic cartridge, occasionally taking the wrong trail, skipping. You just need to give it a little shake and it keeps going, playing this music you can listen to, but that you can also touch. Or at least the needle can touch it, and you can touch the needle, and that's almost the same. And how do you press an instrument — say a trumpet — into the vinyl, so that when the needle goes over it, the trumpet sounds like a trumpet, and not like a dog barking, a vuvuzela, or something else? The (fat) man, the (fat) lady, the (fat) choir, all the orchestra — violins, timbales, trumpets, cellos, instruments with names he ignores, all sounding the way they're supposed to sound, to the best of his knowledge, which isn't much, granted, but he's pretty sure that this trumpet sounds as it should.

It's like that question about the flask: how does the flask know when it has to keep the water cold and when hot? The idea made him laugh.

The place is packed; body odour is the prevalent perfume.

They walk to the bar, rubbing their arms against sweating bodies, then queue for some minutes, their tongues drier than the Atacama Desert. When it's their turn, they order three bottles of beer — from the cold ones, they tell the bartender — and step into the audience to watch the band play. With the loud music taking over Ro finally stops humming the refrain from the overture of *The Flying Dutchman*.

The purveyors of live music are a quintet: drums, bass, two electric guitars, and a singer. They play a slow but heavy tune. The electric guitars are overloaded with effects and sound like anything but guitars. The drummer's sense of tempo is debatable. The bass can't be heard, but then the bass can't ever be heard. The singer — a muscular guy with a crew cut, who's dressed all in black and looks out of place in this band — wails into the microphone. Like everything else, his voice is heavily processed, making it impossible to tell what he sings — perhaps for the best. Maybe it's better if they sound as distant from music as possible. And perhaps it isn't their fault. Perhaps it's too hot for their music to travel through the air in wave form. Maybe their music is now crawling on the floor, dragging along wet tiles and cigarette butts like a sonic slug. They play three songs that could be the same song repeated three times (the record is skipping), and then announce they'll take a break. Few people clap — everyone is either too stoned or too stupefied by the heat to lift their hands. Beli, Ro and Diego head to the bar once more.

"Man, it's boiling in here," says Ro.

"Yes, it is!" says Diego.

"I should have worn shorts," says Ro.

"Do you think that was Nazi music?" asks Beli.

"That wasn't very good… But I don't think it would qualify as Nazi music, no," says Diego.

"And yet…" says Beli.

"And yet what?" says Diego.

"And yet the singer is a well-known skinhead," says Beli, making something up to prove a point.

"He looks like one," says Ro.

"You're talking shit," says Diego.

"No, I'm not," says Beli.

"You can't be a skinhead in this weather! Where have you ever seen one?" says Diego.

"He's one of that band of skinheads who hang out in the skate park by the river," says Beli.

"There's no gang of skinheads in that skate park!" says Diego.

"Oh, yes there is a gang! And that bloke is one of them," says Beli. "A bunch of wankers, the whole lot of them, like all skinheads! But I guess it's easier to worry about Wagner…" he adds. The guy standing to his right turns around and gives Beli a hostile look. Then he walks away. "What was the problem with that one?" asks Beli.

"Either he likes Wagner or he overheard you making stuff up," says Ro.

"I'm not lying…" says Beli.

To avoid queuing once more, they order six more beers. Soon the band resumes playing. The same song from before the break, or another one. Some song. Not the overture from *The Flying Dutchman*.

Der Fliegende Hollander, The Bayreuth Festival Chorus and Orchestra, Joseph Keilberth, 1955. No idea what all of that meant, if they were good, or bad, or meaningless details.

He could only tell that it was an old record. Chances are, all the musicians are dead by now. So in a way, this was like listening to a message from the land of the dead, which added to the strangeness of the needle in its magnetic cartridge, the trumpet that sounded like a trumpet and not like a barking dog or a vuvuzela, the question about the flask knowing when the liquid is cold and when it's hot.

He rescued a joint from the ashtray, pinched the burnt bits away, lit it, took a few drags, and crushed it back into the ashtray.

Of course, you can have a similar experience when you listen to an old CD — this LP must exist as a CD too, after all. But there was something about this gadget, that he couldn't get his head around. He could touch the music, and for that reason the death of the musicians became more palpable. That was deep too — it was, of course, the weed talking. In any case, he felt unsettled by these stupid thoughts. Maybe he just needed to clear his head, get some fresh air.

He pressed stop and went out for a walk.

Now the DJ is playing electronic music. Beli, Diego, and Ro dance manically, covered in sweat from head to toe. There are many pretty girls and boys around — all covered in sweat too — but no need to think about them, because the music and the dance, and the cold beer which makes their temples hurt, and there'll be time for everything else later. Maybe. Because now there's those stroboscopic lights, the epileptic fit always around the corner, so much better than the lights in Beli's hi-fi's EQ, the ones that like to dance to Nazi music.

A FOREIGN COUNTRY IS THE PAST

Perhaps it's because of the lights flashing that Beli doesn't see the large body squaring up to him. A moment later he's on the floor and his face hurts and his hands are wet with other people's sweat, beer, and spit. And next, the three of them are running towards the door, bumping into dancers, chased by five guys. And then there's the exit door, and a bouncer who looks confused as they run past.

Outside it's raining like there's no tomorrow and it's harder to run without slipping everywhere. They make it to the corner, where the chasing party catches up with them. Punches and kicks fly and a bottle lands on Beli's head. The bottle doesn't break but he crashes to the floor again. He feels the rain on his face. Then he feels the punches.

And how the hell had the turntable — and all those LPs full of dead people — ended up in the garbage? Who throws away anything that works these days? Maybe a widow eager to clear space? If this were the case, there would be more records.

The big guy who earlier smashed the bottle on Beli's head now pins him to the floor, while the singer with the cropped hair punches him in the face, punches him in the face, punches him in the face — the record is skipping. Beli tries to turn his face away from the fist, but it's like he has a fist magnet attached to his nose. Diego and Ro watch from a few metres away; when they try to get close to pull Beli to safety, the other four guys — who are standing in a circle with their backs to the singer and Beli — swing their belts at them.

The beating goes on for a minute or two. Suddenly, a clap of thunder announces the storm will get worse. "OK, that's enough," says the big guy, as if taking his cue from the blast. He yanks the singer with the cropped hair away from Beli.

"That will show you making up shit about me!" says the singer. "And you! You better take him away and never turn up again or you'll get it too!" he adds while they walk away.

Diego and Ro help Beli get up. Once on his feet, Beli brings a hand to his nose and blows a blood clot on the floor. He tilts his head to the sky, letting the rain wash his face. He can taste blood in his mouth and trickling down his throat. The taste is strangely appealing.

Beli walked to the bags where he had earlier found the turntable. The newspapers were still there — he hadn't missed any records, or they were already gone. He looked around to see if he could guess where the turntable had come from, but it was impossible to say. He wondered what his father's deck and records had looked like outside, when his mother cleared them out. He grabbed a bunch of newspapers from the pile, just for the sake of taking something back with him.

Back home, he started to go over the new haul. They were all copies of the local newspaper, but a decade old. He looked at the date a few times — checked it against the date in his watch. It's not that they were about a decade old — they were from ten years ago, to the day. This was very odd, but then stranger things happen to those who are stoned.

The newspaper's front page looked slightly different back then, but the layout was pretty much the same

— things do change here, but change crawls, and ten years isn't enough for much to show through. The news didn't differ too much from what you'd find now either, but the police section was slightly slimmer. The only thing that really caught his attention was an article about the raids from that December a lifetime ago. His father had been hooked to the telly all through the raids, worried that they might break into his shop, steal all the machinery, tear the place apart. And they did break in and tear the place apart. And then he was dead — that's how it went. He could read this article and find out more about what the raids were all about, but it wouldn't change a thing.

And the papers smelled damp and old. And they were dust magnets too. He grabbed the whole stack and threw them in the bin. He was about to get rid of the records and the turntable but changed his mind — he wanted to show the new gadget to the guys. He'd sell it all later; there was an antiques shop nearby.

A strange sensation crept up his throat — the feeling that things can always take a turn for the worse. But soon the others would drop by, and they'd smoke weed, and then they'd go to a party, maybe pull someone, and everything would be alright. Everything would be alright. Because you don't always find a record player, you aren't always so lucky. Everything would be alright, because it was Friday. That's all he had to think about right now. The rest was all background noise. Like the scratching sound of an old vinyl.

"Man, this sucks. What the fuck are they doing?" says Beli, holding a sock to his nose. They've been sitting in the A&E

waiting room for hours. The only other person there is a tramp holding a piece of dirty gauze to his head.

"They must be busy with an emergency," says Diego.

"Mine is an emergency too!" says Beli.

"No, it isn't," says Diego.

"Feels like one!" says Beli.

"Does it hurt?" asks Ro, nodding at his nose.

"Yes, it does!" answers Beli.

"Well, you brought it on yourself," says Diego.

"Oh, fuck off!" says Beli.

"No, really… You can't be making up stuff like that… People are sensitive about that kind of thing."

"It was just a joke!" says Beli. "Plus, if he isn't a Nazi he acts like one," he adds.

"Yes, that's true," agrees Ro.

"How long do you reckon we're going to be here?" asks Diego.

"I've got no idea," says Beli.

"Well, there's only that wino there… But he was here before us… So, who knows?" says Ro.

"You two can go home," says Beli.

"Nah, I'm staying here with you," says Ro.

"Yeah, me too," says Diego.

Ro starts humming the refrain from the Overture of *The Flying Dutchman*. Diego is about to tell him to stop singing Nazi music, but instead, he starts humming along too. Beli joins them.

"Shut the fuck up!" says the old drunk.

And that's exactly what they do. The three of them slur to the low zones, as if someone had pressed the stop button.

OWL

They drive slowly past the roadside shrine and Cynthia catches a glimpse of all the bottles shimmering in the sun. There are many more than last summer. Why would anyone bring them here, who is the shrine consecrated to? She doesn't know. But then you can't always make sense of this kind of thing. She should bring her own bottle one day, just to be on the safe side.

As she wraps up these thoughts that momentarily rescue her from the monotony of the two-hour journey, the car takes a right turn and enters the narrow dirt road that ends in the farmhouse. While they roll along under a grove of poplars, Cynthia recalls that her grandmother told her of another shrine nearby — people seem to have a thing for them around this neck of the woods. This one is consecrated to four teenagers who died in an accident sixty or so years ago, when their car fell in a ditch. This is nothing special, since car accidents are the number one killer for young people in the countryside. But it turns out that the boy who was driving the car was dating her Grandma at the time. That her grandmother might have had a boyfriend at some point in her life, and that this boyfriend wasn't her grandfather, was hard to process. But the hardest thing to process was the thought of drowning in a car, miles from the nearest river or lake, and half a day from the sea.

And now they don't end up in a ditch but go through a gate that's been left open in anticipation of their arrival. A short while later, the car stops outside the farmhouse.

Cynthia pokes Leo to wake him up and they get out in silence. Her father follows them out, and then walks to the trunk and gets the bags and the shotgun out. He sets the luggage down while the wind carries the sound of dogs. Puig — no known first name — is approaching in the distance, black beret pulled low over his eyes, taking long strides in his rubber boots, carrying a folder in his left hand, followed by four excited mutts. When he's some ten metres away, he extends his right arm and continues to walk with his arm outstretched. Her father starts walking towards Puig with his arm extended too. For a few seconds, they walk in a meeting course with arms jutting out, almost as if they were the International Space Station, and a shuttle, performing a complex coupling manoeuvre in low Earth orbit. Finally their hands clasp, and as they shake, a fast conversation unfolds about the food waiting in the fridge (Puig refuses to say how much he's spent), the documents Puig needs her father to sign (which explain the folder he's carrying), her mother not coming this time (the gate can be locked), Puig's family (wife now working as a cleaner, girl doing well in school, boy is trouble, as always), the hot weather (her father: has Puig left the windows open to let the morning air in?; Puig: yes, but close them before it gets hotter outside), and the drought (Puig: the crops could do with some rain; her father: it's hotter than in other years). An uncomfortable silence interrupts the conversation. Then Puig surrenders the folder, waves at everyone with a slight tip of his beret, and starts walking back to his lodge.

The dogs follow him and don't stop barking and who knows if they ever will.

The farmhouse was built towards the turn of the century. It isn't that big compared to some of the others around — just four bedrooms, a large kitchen, dining room, and an integrated lounge. It could do with a bit of painting and gas heating on top of the salamander, but it's like stepping back into another time — a time when things were simpler, as her father says every time he fires the salamander after a minor struggle, and starts reminiscing about his childhood, which must have been quite cold in winter. Not that they need heating right now — right now it'd be good to have a bit of AC, and, of course, the house doesn't have that either.

As usual, Cynthia gets the bedroom on the top floor, Leo the one at the back, and her father the double bedroom by the front door. After the rooms are distributed, Cynthia realises it's the first time they're here since her grandmother died, that one room will remain empty. That her mother stayed at home with a migraine makes more sense now. As much as they disliked each other, they still needed one another, if only to argue over every single detail, from the size of the tomatoes in the salad, to how long the kids should stay indoors after lunch, to how her father likes his steak, to when to water the plants, and so on.

Cynthia opens the wardrobe to arrange the few clothes she's brought, but the stench of damp pushes her back. She leaves the clothes in the bag and sets it on the chair. Then she lays down on the bed, her arms folded behind her head.

She's walking over cracked land, carrying a shimmering bottle of water. The shrine can be seen in the distance, and her grandmother is waiting for her there. It's sunny but there are also clouds and the sky is rumbling. A bolt of lightning cuts across the sky, and she drops her bottle, which bounces on the hard ground, almost as if it were made of rubber. The bottle bounces over and over, until it bounces against a rock and breaks, and her grandmother screams, and the scream feels very close. Then Leo is kissing her neck and sticking his finger in her ear. She pushes him away, curses him, and Leo leaves the room laughing. She sits down and looks at her watch on the night table: it's already twelve o'clock. She's slept for over two hours.

She walks into the kitchen. Her father and Leo are sitting at the table, eating, and reading the paper. Her father is already half-through a bottle of wine. Cynthia sits with them and grabs a piece of bread. She cuts a slice of salami and some cheese. She watches them eat, mouths open, food visible, both chewing noisily.

"You are a retard..." she finally spits at Leo.

"Cynthia!" says her father.

"He was being weird again!" says Cynthia, and Leo breaks into a fit of laughter.

A FOREIGN COUNTRY IS THE PAST

"Leo!" says her father, and Leo kicks Cynthia under the table. "Leo!" says her father, now louder.

"What have I done now?" asks Leo.

"You're such a waste of air..." says Cynthia and Leo giggles again.

She grabs the Saturday supplement. She isn't interested in reading it — she just needs a curtain to hide behind.

After lunch Leo leaves the house carrying the shotgun and starts shooting as soon as he's got one foot out; her father stumbles to his room for a nap. Cynthia exits too, to go and read her magazine in the shade, under the grapevine. It's hot and there are storm clouds forming in the distance; there's a weak breeze that carries the smell of rain and manure. Like in her dream, there's the sound of thunder, here — in real life — providing a counterpoint to Leo's gun. It's as if Leo and the thunder took turns to make their noise. But it's more likely that it's Leo who waits for the moments of silence to shoot, so that everyone within audible distance knows he might be an idiot, but he's an idiot with a gun.

Cynthia reads an article about the summer at the seaside. "Reading" is perhaps an overstatement, since the "article" is mainly a collage of photos of tanned people dressed in pastel colours, smiling for the camera, plus some telegraphic captions. Celebrities, socialites, politicians, models, businessmen, actors, the usual. The parties are in houses, nightclubs, five star hotels, five star restaurants. Everyone is happy, their mouths full of shiny teeth. They always publish this type of tripe during the summer break;

it must be so that normal people have someone to hate, and don't think so much about their own lives. But the photos have the opposite effect on her, because they make her think about her own summer, so far spent mainly in their flat, and now in this damp and depressing farmhouse. And because she thinks of this summer, she starts to think about all summers: she can't remember the last time they went on a proper holiday. Was it when she was five or six, and they went to the seaside and it rained non-stop, and she got food poisoning from eating fried whitebait in an old restaurant in the harbour? It was full of fishing boats and sea lions and she can still smell them; she has connected their smell with food poisoning ever since. Why have they never been on holiday again? It's not that they can't afford it. Perhaps her parents are embarrassed about Leo. Such an unnecessary hassle, Leo. No one could have guessed how he'd turn out, but he was an unnecessary complication. And all her mother's fault. At least she should be here dealing with him. And when they're back in town, it'll be her father's turn to disappear with some rubbish excuse, not a migraine but some made-up work-related trip. And look at all these morons smiling for the camera! What the hell are they so happy about?

Cynthia puts the magazine down and at that exact moment, a shot rings in the air. A millisecond later, thunder. Both sound near.

Leo arrives carrying a massive dead bird from its feet. When he gets to the fence that divides the farmhouse from the fields, he spreads it from the wings and leaves it hanging from the wiring, like an avian Jesus Christ. He walks slowly towards Cynthia, shotgun slung over his left shoulder like a Partisan, and sits in a chair under the grapevine. He wipes his nose using the bottom of his T-shirt. He stares at Cynthia.

"Seen this?" he says, eventually.

"I'm not interested," says Cynthia.

"One shot. Just one shot."

"Good for you."

"It isn't easy to shoot a bird with just one shot..."

"I'm not interested!"

"Oh, well, whatever!" says Leo. He gets up and heads inside.

Here Cynthia finally lifts her eyes and sees the dead bird clearly: its wings stretch more than a metre and half; its huge dead eyes are wide open, staring straight ahead. Such a big bird hanging dead from the wiring is a sad sight — what was the point of shooting it? She'll never understand that mindless compulsion to kill. Not that she's an animal lover or anything close to it, but wasting time shooting things just doesn't make sense to her.

Behind the bird, in the distance, thunder and dark clouds and a lighting bolt. In the distance as well, but closer, Puig approaches in his boots, taking his usual long strides, his black beret pulled all the way down to his eyes, followed by just one of his loud dogs this time. He cuts across the field, goes under the wire, and then walks up the path, until he finally reaches the dead bird and stops before it. He studies it for a few seconds, moving his head from side to side. Then he turns towards the grapevine, and when he sees Cynthia he nods to acknowledge her presence, his usual smile absent. He removes his beret and pushes it against his chest — he seems saddened by the dead bird. Cynthia feels that she needs to go and say something and she walks towards him. The dog stops barking, as if to let her speak.

"Leo shot it," she says when she reaches Puig.

"It's a pity," says Puig. "These things kill mice. We're full of mice round here. Mice everywhere, even with the drought. And we've had a few cases of hemorrhagic fever. He shouldn't shoot owls, no. There are other things to shoot. Lots of things to shoot round here."

"You know how he is..." says Cynthia, taking her right finger to her right temple and tapping a couple of times. "I'll speak to my father when he wakes up. Maybe he can take his gun away."

"No need for that. He can shoot all the pigeons and partridges he wants. He can shoot hare — there's a lot of hare — vermin. But not these owls. There aren't that many owls left and we're full of mice, and then there's the fever..." he repeats, replacing his beret on his head. "And of course: it's bad luck to shoot an owl," he adds.

"I'm sorry, really... I'll let them know," says Cynthia, feeling guilty for a crime she hasn't committed.

"Thank you, Cynthia," says Puig, and a flash of lightning first, and a second later a loud clap of thunder, announce the rain, buckets of it, all at once.

Puig nods at her and then bolts towards his lodge, holding the beret over his head. The mutt runs behind him, barking once again. Cynthia runs towards the farmhouse, and when she reaches the door, she turns around to watch the dead owl. It's raining so hard that it seems to be moving. It is moving. But it's probably moving because of the rain.

A FOREIGN COUNTRY IS THE PAST

The storm has been raging for an hour when the rain and thunder stop abruptly, like someone flipped a switch. At that moment, her father and Leo walk into the kitchen.

"I'll make some coffee," says her father. "That was some storm, wasn't it?"

"Yes, it was… By the way, Puig dropped by to complain about this one," she says, pointing at Leo with the magazine folded into a tube.

"What did I do?"

"You shot an owl, that's what you did," she says.

"So?" asks Leo.

"Puig said you shouldn't shoot owls when you can shoot other birds. Or hares."

"And why can't I shoot an owl? It was in our plot."

"Because owls eat mice, and there aren't many owls left, and something about some fever. And bad luck. That's what Puig said."

"Puig's right. Shoot something else next time," says her father.

"What does Puig know?" asks Leo.

"Well, he's lived all his life here, so he must know a thing or two," says Cynthia.

"That's depressing," says Leo.

"Just shoot something else, Leo," insists her father.

"Whatever," says Leo.

Soon the smell of coffee fills the air. Cynthia would love a cup, but instead she walks out of the kitchen and heads to her room. She opens the curtains and looks out of the window. The owl isn't there any more. Either Puig took it down, or one of the dogs or some other animal snatched it. Or it came back to life, and flew away, like the avian Jesus

Christ it was. She lies on the bed, staring at the ceiling with her arms folded behind her head. The damp stains on the ceiling look like the map of an undiscovered continent. She can even see the rivers in it. She starts to follow one of them from one corner of the ceiling to the opposite end.

But soon Leo's shooting restarts and she's forcefully removed from her riverine revery. Here she thinks that it would be great if he accidentally shot himself in the head and died. He could jump over a fence while he's out there killing defenceless animals, the shotgun could accidentally fall on its butt, bang, get him in the right temple. Game Over. Accidents like this happen all the time in the countryside. It'd be totally unexpected, one of those moments when the fabric of reality breaks, and things change forever from one second to the next. Leo would be late for dinner, and sooner or later her father would go and get Puig to arrange a search party. They'll head out with torches, and with the help of the dogs, they'd find him in a corner of the plot, lying dead, with one clean shot to the head, as clean as birdshot can be. Then there'll be the funeral with a closed casket, and her mother and father would be sad for a month or two, they'd cry a lot, but then life would go on, and eventually no one would mention Leo again, like it happened with her grandmother. Then they might even go on a summer holiday again.

One shot, that's all it would take. One shot. And the owls would certainly love it.

When she comes down, there's no sign of her father or Leo in the kitchen. She heads out and scans the fields around the house and they aren't out there either. The gate is open but the car is still parked at the front garden, so they can't be far.

She walks to the car, finds the keys waiting for her in the ignition, gets in. She rearranges the seat to her height, decides against wearing the seatbelt, starts the engine, and drives slowly in reverse until she crosses the gate. Here she turns right to take the dirt road in the opposite direction from which they arrived. When she's driving away from the house, she can spot them in the distance, following a path that ends in a thicket of eucalyptuses; her father is carrying the shotgun and Leo is swinging an unrecognisable dead animal. She feels a pang of sadness, not for the dead animal, but for them. They look so small in the distance, framed against the giant trees. No shotgun could remedy that.

She drives slowly and the wheels make a soothing sound when they roll over the wet dirt. She doesn't know where she's driving to — she only knows that she needs to drive. Luckily there's no mud and she can focus on the landscape instead of having to worry about staying on the road. But the landscape is flat and boring — just soy fields and trees all around — and soon she wishes there was at least a moderate level of risk involved in the operation, something to keep her entertained. And here she realises that she's driving in the direction of the shrine her grandmother mentioned — the one for the drowned teenagers. Her Grandma said it's on this dirt road, after the abandoned windmill, by a grove of poplars. She remembers that spot; not the poplars — there are millions of them, nothing but poplars — but she does remember the old windmill. And soon there they are, the windmill and the poplars, just a few metres away. There's no sign of the ditch where they drowned — they must have covered it up after the accident.

She parks the car by a narrow overgrown trail. She gets out and walks towards the trail, passing the rusty windmill. One of its vanes is hanging loosely and squeaking, looking ready to drop; she wishes she were a giant, that she could pull it like a wobbly tooth. She keeps walking and just before the grove, in a small round clearing, she finds it: a thick wooden plank with a large cross in the middle. There are names etched on it, but they are illegible, destroyed by the sun and the weather and the years. She wonders how many times her grandmother was here, if she saw the names disappear, or if she stopped coming before that happened. There are dry flowers scattered about and random rubbish, including several used condoms, crushed cans of Coca Cola, and a latex glove. And perched atop a large wooden pole that seems to serve no purpose, there's an owl staring down at her. She should be spooked, but the way it moves its head and watches her intently is oddly reassuring. And it's a beautiful animal, especially now that it's alive. She feels like it could fly away at any time, and for the second time today, she feels the need to apologise for someone else's crime.

"I'm sorry he killed you," she says and the bird tilts its head. "He's unwell…" The bird turns its head once more, hoots a couple of times, then takes off. Cynthia watches it disappear, and then walks into the grove: more rubbish — more condoms, more empty cans of Coca Cola, more latex gloves, an empty oil can, leftovers of a portable cooler, remains of a burnt tyre, and that's about it. There's nothing to keep her here, so she walks back to the car, gets in, and stays watching the hanging vane move in the breeze, until she's satisfied it won't fall today. Then she drives back to the farmhouse.

When she arrives Leo and her father are still out. They'll still be out a couple of hours later, when night falls, and the mosquitoes come out for dinner. They'll be out while she fixes herself a salad and finishes the bottle of wine, opens a new one and downs half, so her father won't notice the missing drink. They'll be out when she goes to bed and falls asleep right away, dizzy but at peace with the world.

And then the owl is banging its head against the window, is banging its head against the wall, is banging its head against the wardrobe, is banging its head against the bed, is banging its head against a giant glass bottle, as it tries to fly out of the room. On and on banging — the noise is unbearable. And there are feathers flying in the air, and the white walls of her room are all stained with blood. And the owl keeps banging against the windows, and it keeps banging like a fly, and at times the owl is her Grandma, other times the owl is her mother, other times it's Leo, and the noise gets louder, and the glass will eventually break. And suddenly she stops trying to help the owl out, and comes back to her room, to her bed, and she's covered in sweat, her head hurts, and her mouth tastes like stale wine. It takes her a few moments to realise someone is knocking on the door downstairs.

She turns the light on and sits on the bed. She checks the time and it's one-seventeen in the morning, and the knocks don't stop, and they seem to be getting louder. Something must have happened — maybe Leo did die in the end. Or maybe not. Maybe her father and Leo just forgot to take the keys with them. She should head downstairs, and at least see who's at the door, decide whether she'll open or not later. But she can't leave her bed. It wouldn't be safe to leave now, not with an owl loose in the room. So she turns the lights off, covers her head with the sheets, and lies down again.

And like this she stays, hoping the knocks will soon end. And if they don't, that she'll fall asleep again anyway.

COLOUR THEORY

O glorioso Martire San Gennaro

Humidity kills. That's what everyone usually says when they've run out of more interesting things to talk about. It might be small talk, but it's also true. And December is the most likely time of the year to die like this. The pressure increases as the calendar sheds weight, the numbers on the barometer keep climbing, and it feels like your lungs could implode. Until one night the sky starts to rumble, and there it arrives, the storm. And with the storm comes a bit of relief. And suddenly you can breathe again. But soon along comes the flood too: the traffic grinds to a halt, people get crushed by falling trees, or drown when they're sucked in by an open manhole. And a day or two later the cycle restarts, with the pressure growing, the storm arriving after a few weeks, a bit mellower each time, up to the time when leaves are yellow, and the torrential rains have turned to drizzle. Peace for a while — autumn first, then a short winter, then a relatively pleasant spring. But summer returns the following year and it all bursts in December once again.

There's something Sisyphean about it, but then there's something Sisyphean about everything.

Ninety-eight percent humidity now, according to the woman on the radio. The storm has been lurking above for over ten days. It nearly hit last Friday, but in the end it was just a quick shower, and the relief and the flood never came. Now the humidity is close to one hundred percent — how is that even possible? Throw thirty-seven degrees into the equation, and it's enough to drive people and animals insane. Things go insane too. The papers on the table are damp and the pieces of coursework, which should be dry by now, are also damp and stain one another and his chronically dirty fingers. The work shirt sticks to his back, and the jeans stick to his legs. And the dark cigarettes stink worse than usual, and the smoke splashes on the floor, instead of creeping upwards towards the ceiling. Even sounds sound different — louder, sharper, the horns of the passing cars hurt his ears, the engines bounce against the furniture, and he can even hear the walls moan as they struggle to breathe; or at least he can see them sweating and imagines the rattle of the fan is their breath. Of course this kind of weather could kill you.

That is, of course, if you don't get killed by something else. So many options to choose from; the older you get the worse it is — life turns into a bazaar of death. But you don't even need to be old to die — see what happened to those two young girls who got run over last Friday. Those deaths stayed with him and perhaps stayed with everyone, because they've been talking about them non-stop on the radio and the telly and the paper — so much they've made everyone forget about different ways of dying, even death by humidity. Drunk drivers kill, that's what everyone must be saying now in the supermarket queue, when they're out of more interesting things to talk about.

And here we go again, a relative on the radio, mouthing something barely comprehensible with that south-side accent, that accent that betrays slaughterhouses and the steel factory where once he tried to organise a cell with Polo. That must have been in '73 or '74, in another life, back when they still thought they could change the world. The relative is choking on tears, wailing about the dead girls, the fugitive driver, and the injustice of it all. It takes time to realise that the nature of things is injustice. The sooner you understand that, the better. This poor man still needs to figure it out.

She arranged the tubes, the palette, the brushes, and the little glasses with water and turpentine on the table and got ready to disappear in the exercise. When she was a kid she'd spend hours playing with her watercolours — she could remember dissolving for hours. The persistence of that memory is how she knew which way to go after school. No matter how many times her grandmother had tried to put her off, saying she should study medicine, law, business management, something useful, that she was the first in the family to go to university, that she had a duty to do well. That stubborn woman, banging on about how they'd been hungry back in Naples when they were kids, how she, on the other hand, would never know what it's like to be hungry, because she'd never lived through a war, but maybe she would find out, maybe she would, if she didn't do something useful with her life, and on, and on. It was pointless to argue with her. Her parents had been a bit more forthcoming, but still hadn't been able to hide their disappointment, asking if she planned to study "something else on the side." They all meant well but she didn't have to listen to them or anyone else. Life's too short to waste it away doing what other people want you to do.

The task at hand now was to take a certain colour on a trip. That's how the old professor had described it. "Look, it's easy: you just need to take a colour on a trip." Before he'd tell you what colour you'd travel with; this time she had to choose her own. But whether you chose your own colour or he assigned you one, you had to provide a flow within the allocated number of steps, and create something that felt like a coherent progression rather than a random game of chromatic hopscotch.

"A trip. That's what it is. But it has to be a nice relaxing cruise in the Mediterranean and not a bumpy train ride," the professor had said, with overdone poetic intention.

They crossed the avenue without looking, and even if they had looked, they would've missed the speeding car anyway — it was coming at them too fast to register. They were scooped up onto the hood, and the car kept going past the avenue until it reached the far corner, where the driver slammed on the brakes and sent them flying. Here they traced a downward-facing parabolic trajectory of about fifteen metres, and landed against the concrete. They were still rolling on the road when he ran them over and vanished into the night. The whole thing must have taken ten seconds, twelve at most.

A FOREIGN COUNTRY IS THE PAST

Not that it adds anything to the incident, but when this happened the barometer was stuck on ninety-four percent. A few minutes later, with the bodies still warm, there was thunder and finally there it was, the rain. It washed their blood off the road and into the gutter, saving the street cleaners from some unpleasant work. But just as suddenly as it came, the rain was gone. A simulacrum of a storm. Or a storm that dropped by just to wash their blood away, if you are one of those who believe things happen for a reason.

Ninety-four percent and very hot. You'd think things would melt in this weather, but the road was as hard as usual. Humidity, which makes clothes, paper, walls, everything damp, doesn't liquify concrete. A pity for the two girls, because if the road had been liquid, then the car might have spared them, as long as they'd known how to swim.

che, con l'esercizio continuo di tutte le virtù cristiane, attendeste alla santificazione del gregge affidato al vostro zelo pastorale e di quanti vi conobbero

The Mediterranean cruise — the final piece of coursework of the year. Only rules: same primary colour, from its lightest to its darkest hue, in twenty gradual steps. It sounded straightforward, nothing impossible if you had a bit of patience and attention to detail. And yet there was always a jolt here or there — a hue too light or too dark. It'd been a bumpy ride for her so far, judging by the crosses the old professor had left in the margins of all her previous submissions.

And here an idea occurred to her. Perhaps the best way to go about it was to work the progression towards the lighter tones, and then towards the dark ones, in separate mixes, on the palette. In this way she'd be able to observe the whole flow before she transferred it as a whole to the paper. Like this she wouldn't have to repaint the thing four hundred times, until she ended up giving up. So that was it? It felt almost too simple to be right. But then the simplest things are the easiest to overlook.

She pressed the tube and a little red worm crawled on the palette. Then she pressed the white tube. Then she pressed the black tube. Then she started working on the mixes.

Israel is incredibly dry, most of the Middle East is. And like most of the Middle East, Israel is quite yellow too. Unless you happen to be inland, where you can find some green spots. By the sea, the prevalent colours are yellow and blue, plus the white and beige of the houses and buildings.

By contrast, there are some places in other parts of the world that can be humid for long stretches of time. Say in Europe — there are several humid places in Europe. These humid places often lean towards the green, like Ireland, Wales, parts of England. Not Amsterdam. Amsterdam is humid but not necessarily green. Instead, the prevailing colours in Amsterdam are brown, gold and white. Amsterdam has an average relative humidity of eighty-two point five percent.

Do they say that humidity kills in Amsterdam? Or do they get murdered by something else?

A FOREIGN COUNTRY IS THE PAST

Of course they'll never find him. It's so easy to get out of here, leaving no traces at all. He never tried it because he thought he'd manage to stay underground until things cooled down, since he wasn't necessarily a big fish, and they had no reasons to search for him. Obviously he should have taken off — it would have spared him and others a lot of grief. Just jump on the ferry across the river, or walk across the Triple Border, where no one ever asks any questions, and if they ask, you can always answer with a wad of notes. Once in another country, you buy a new identity — there's a market for that, like there's a market for everything. Then you disappear, in the positive sense of the term, not theirs. Many got out like this.

Later, some of them returned to join the Counteroffensive, carrying along their new names, new haircuts, perms for the ladies, short hair for the gentlemen, no suspicious beards, no reading glasses, should they look too intellectual, no compromising literature, no literature at all — they were completely different people, unrecognisable, even their kids had different names and birthdays. The problem is that a new identity can't buy the silence of the snitches; in the end it all came down to them, the snitches. And yes, snitches might have a lot to answer for in this mess, but history is also cruel to them. Because if you haven't been on the receiving end of a cattle prod, then you shouldn't have an opinion on this matter. What the hell would you know about anything if you haven't had fifteen thousand volts running through your cunt or balls? But those were other times, and this fugitive is different — the kind of fugitive who doesn't get caught. Not because he isn't important but because no one important has anything to gain from finding him. The kind of fugitive who doesn't get the cattle prod if they accidentally bump into him.

He wipes his hands with the ragged tea towel, grabs the cigarettes from the table, taps the pack a few times against his knee, and keeps tapping, perhaps to avoid noticing that his right hand is shaking.

She waved her hand to scare off the little black flies. They were hovering about dangerously close to the palette, while red and black blended in an homogenous dark mass that resembled black pudding, or the coagulated blood of San Gennaro, the patron saint of Naples. His blood — stored in two ampules within a silver reliquary — liquifies (or doesn't) three times a year, in a phenomenon no one has been able to explain yet — a phenomenon completely unrelated to the drill she was supposed to complete. On the other hand, the liquefaction of San Gennaro's blood might (or might not) have something to do with Naples' humidity, which isn't that high — an average of sixty-eight point thirty-three percent a year — but it's higher in the months when the liquefaction happens (or doesn't): May, September, and December. During those months, San Gennaro's blood can metamorphose from a black pudding-like substance into a dark red liquid — aka blood.

Maybe that September 16, 1980, when the blood failed to liquefy, it was unusually dry, and for that reason, the miracle didn't take place? Who knows? In any case, two months after this unsuccessful liquefaction there was that earthquake in Naples — the one that killed over three thousand, including some of her distant relatives. But a month later she was born, eleven thousand two hundred and twenty-six kilometres away from San Gennaro's black pudding, in a different continent, in a different hemisphere, in a different language, in a very humid place. Her grandmother lit a candle to the patron saint and prayed for her first grandchild and prayed for her family back in Naples too: the Lord giveth and the Lord taketh away.

Not that she was thinking of any of this while she was mixing red and black. Saints think for themselves, or the faithful think on their behalf. She wasn't a believer and she didn't care about San Gennaro, whether his blood would liquefy in two days or not. She only had a mind for her trip with colour. She needed to get it right this time. She needed the Mediterranean cruise. But whoever plays with red paint plays with blood. And that blood — unless it's San Gennaro's or black pudding — is generally liquid.

voi, che suggellaste, col vostro sangue generoso, la fede di Gesù Cristo su questo colle, dove ogni anno vive il segno prodigioso del vostro martirio e del vostro valido patrocinio

On the days that followed the accident, there was nothing else on the radio, the TV, or in the papers — nothing but the two dead girls. And their faces were plastered everywhere, because the public loves the dead, especially when the dead are young. Photos of them during their high school graduation ceremony the year before, with their matching electric blue dresses. Photos of them in preschool. Photos of them during a school trip. Photos of them in all sorts of situations, in all sorts of places, with all sorts of people; a young but long friendship, the future unwritten, and now there wasn't a future any longer — ten seconds or so was all it took for the future to vanish. A few days later a grainy black-and-white photo started to compete with the images of the dead girls — a photo of the driver. Surrounded by officers while being escorted into the police station, his expression the expression of someone who knows very well he's crossed a threshold to a place from which there's no return. Not necessarily an expression of guilt, but one that betrayed the realisation that things would never be the same again.

There was only one photo of him — that's all the local papers managed. And then he absconded, that same week, after being released on bail by a lenient judge. He didn't escape on a ferry or via the Triple Border. Instead he escaped with his actual passport, on a flight from the capital to Istanbul. Later, he might have been spotted in Tel Aviv. And some years later, he was captured in Amsterdam. But the Dutch slept on the extradition and he ran away once more. And he was never seen again.

A single photo, ubiquitous, reproduced non-stop, when everyone was so hungry for more images. And everyone was left hungry, because you can't photograph those who are missing, no matter how hard you try.

It wasn't a coincidence that she'd chosen red. She'd chosen red without thinking but artists think in unconscious ways. Yes, she was already an artist. Sooner or later she'd figure out why she had chosen red, but right now it didn't matter. Now she just needed to get on with that cruise on the Mediterranean.

Everyone likes to believe that when you live as a fugitive, you live looking back. Looking back towards the place you've left behind, but also physically looking back, in case you're being followed. Everyone likes to believe that a life lived like this makes no sense at all.

But the truth is that eventually everything becomes a habit: looking back, being away from those you love, even that feeling of having crossed a threshold towards a place of no return. We live our lives on autopilot — it's no different for fugitives. So when he takes a table at an outdoors café in the Quartieri Spagnoli, that area of Naples where the dominant colours are grey and beige, he will look back, but only to check if the waiter is anywhere near. And when he spots the waiter, he'll wave at him. And the waiter will come to his table, smiling at a face he knows quite well.

"Buon giorno, Paolo," the waiter will say.

"Salve, Romano," Pablo will reply.

Tonight he'll wear the light-blue shirt.

Light-blue is a good colour for this hot weather, without being white, which is so dirty, or at least he's too dirty for it, since he ends up full of wine or food stains every time he wears a white shirt. And light-blue is also a good choice, because with any darker blue, he'd end up with sweat marks under the armpits. Also, he doesn't want to look like a policeman. That's what the guys would say if he wore dark blue — they love repeating the same jokes and he doesn't want to give them any ammo.

Everyone who isn't dead or missing will be there tonight, as every year, when they meet to celebrate their own version of Christmas. Some games of billiards on one of the last good tables still standing, and then a few beers, wine, lots of smoking, arguments that will grow in intensity as the beers and the wine flow. Then someone who had one too many might call him a coward for not joining the Counteroffensive. Then in a drunken stupor, perhaps accuse him directly of being the one who shopped Polo and Claudia. Maybe they even have an attempt at a fisticuff. It'd be a very unfortunate scene.

It has never happened before, someone calling him a snitch. And it might not happen tonight either. But he won't stop both fearing and hoping it eventually happens. And he'll still be going next year, if he's still around, because he does owe it to Polo and Claudia to be there. At least he owes them the possibility of that uncomfortable moment.

But the mix for the final stop in the cruise had to be darker than this, darker than black pudding, or San Gennaro's coagulated blood, which she wasn't thinking about. She added more black but maybe she had overdone it, since now it was hard to distinguish the red from the black. She could already see the old professor's expression of disgust when he corrected her submission, the smirk on his face when he grabbed the blue biro with his stained right hand, in order to cross out the box with the black pudding red slash black mix, his ecstasy when he'd write "too dark!" in the right margin. Still, she'd use it. First, because it might lighten when it settled on the paper; second, because it was already getting late, and Julia would soon come and pick her up to go and buy that dress they'd seen yesterday — that lovely red summer dress that she'd wear when they went out this weekend. So that's why she had chosen red! But now it was still Wednesday and she should focus on getting this done, submit it before they broke for the summer.

She mixed the acrylic paint with her small hard brush, just two or three more spins, and now the whole progression was ready on the palette — it looked better than ever before. Then she started transferring the paint to the paper, cleaning the brush with turpentine and water after each step. And suddenly she was filling the remaining little box with her black pudding red and black. That was it: the cruise's final destination. At this exact moment, one of the small fruit flies messing about crashed against the palette and stayed there, choking with the paint, moving less and less until it didn't move any more. She didn't spot it, and ended up accidentally lifting it with the brush and painting it onto the page, when she was hastily retouching the darkest box for a final time.

otteneteci la grazia di praticare fedelmente i nostri doveri cristiani, di confessare generosamente la verità, di amare sempre Gesù, per assicurarci con la vostra protezione, la gloria eterna del Paradiso. Amen.

And like that, nothing happened that year.

The waiter will bring Paolo a ristretto and a small glass of water. Pablo will be reading in the paper an article about how San Gennaro's blood liquified the previous day, December 16, 2022. Although "reading" might not be the best way to describe it, because he'll mostly look at the pictures. Occasionally a word will seem familiar, but it'll get lost in the sea of other words he won't make sense of. So he'll never find out that the blood occasionally liquifies in the presence of the Pope. Or that sometimes the blood doesn't liquify, and bad things happen, like in 1980, with that earthquake. Or that other times it liquifies, and bad things happen anyway. Or that other times it doesn't liquify and nothing happens at all. They should really take care of all the paedophiles in the church, instead of messing about in those silly costumes, he'll think, while the waiter approaches the table to ask him if he'd like anything else.

Here Pablo will order a glass of red wine. Eleven-fifteen in the morning and he'll be ordering wine. And why not? He won't know why he'll feel like drinking red wine so early, but that he chose red wine this time of the year isn't a coincidence.

Soon the waiter will bring the glass of red wine and rest it on the table. Pablo will have a sip from the glass, unaware that he'll be drinking blood, that anyone who drinks red wine ultimately drinks blood. And when he goes to place the glass on the table he'll place it on a crease in the tablecloth; the glass will almost tip over, and some drops of blood will stain the white tablecloth. But the red from the wine will just be red wine to Pablo, not blood. It'll always be just red wine and nothing else. He'll make no connection with anything else. No connection with San

A FOREIGN COUNTRY IS THE PAST

Gennaro. And no connection with that other red — that red dress on his windscreen, almost twenty-five years ago. He'll make sure the wine hasn't stained his clothes. Then he'll get up, leave a ten euro note under the glass and walk away. Then he'll live the rest of his life. And everyday will follow the previous one. Until his days run out.

The old professor turns the radio off, walks to the window, and opens the curtains. He can barely feel the breeze coming in; and yet the breeze is in the room, rattling the papers on the table. For a second he fears they'll fly off, but the papers are instead kept in place by the acrylic paint that has liquified like the blood of that saint whose name he can't remember. He lights another of his stinky dark cigarettes, has a long drag that makes him slightly dizzy, watches the ash drop on the floor, sits on his stool and grabs the first submission, which could very well be one from the middle, and it could be the one at the bottom. They're all different, they are all unique, but they're all the same, because they don't get it. OK, at some point in Colour Theory 2 they get better at this kind of drill, but they'll never really understand colour, and this is very sad.

Mediocrity is what they are — a form of chromatic centrism. It's not that he enjoys this mediocrity; it's that he can't spell it to them — he can't spell it or he'll ruin it for them. He hated these drills, of course, everyone does, because they are the admin of painting. But then he understood how colour holds the universe together, much like atoms, or the twelve-tone scale in music, which you can find everywhere, even in the way planets are connected with one another, like whatever his name wrote, something with G, or O, that guy from the Caucasus who was fashionable back in the day. And this epiphany — how colour holds the universe together — the moment he figured it out, is one of the few happy memories he has kept, possibly the only one. It happened once when they were smoking weed with Polo. It must have been at Claudia's house, he can't be sure, and it suddenly dawned on him that colour held everything together; he was reading that guy from the Caucasus then, and he clocked it, the penny dropped: it was the same as with music. And he tried to explain it to Polo, but poor Polo was too much into the Frankfurt School to be open to anything remotely metaphysical. Of course he didn't get it, and instead started laughing, called him a hippy, and they both laughed and laughed, and Claudia came from the kitchen and joined them. She wasn't stoned, nor did she know what the joke was about, but she laughed too. And their laughter must have gone on for minutes — it was as if they had disappeared into it. This was before Polo found out about him and Claudia — before they had a fight and never talked to each other again. And it happened before the cattle prod, and what came after, needless to say, but he doesn't even want to go there, doesn't want to think about all of that now, because soon he'll meet the others, and then he'll have no choice but to think about Polo and Claudia and the cattle prod. So he better keep marking this crap.

He marks two, three, four, five, all either green or yellow, lots of things to improve, plenty of angry notes, not really about the submissions, but the submissions come in handy. And now there's this red page that jumps in front of his eyes, a break from tepid colours. He starts to follow the hues from light to dark, and finally a place to let his thoughts evaporate. It's a nice flow, there's something delicate and yet powerful about it. The colour travels well, it moves from one box to the next coherently — nice red flow. Now this here is obviously the red straight out of the tube, and it has to be that brand he hates, he can't remember the name either, but it still travels well in both directions, even in spite of that horrible brand of paint, which isn't even the cheapest one. He leaves ticks outside each one of the boxes and doing it feels surprisingly uplifting. Until he gets to the darkest box. What's this lump? What's this lump of paint here? He removes the lid from the back of his biro and uses the tail to scratch the paper, and with the scratching motion, a dead insect comes into view. It looks like one of those flies that are everywhere right now. Yes, it's one of those flies. He ponders for a few seconds whether he should leave a note reminding the student not to include dead insects with her coursework, but he doesn't — perhaps because he doesn't want to ruin his brief moment of communion with colour. He gives it a good mark, and that's it, that's the last one for now.

He gets his light-blue shirt from the wardrobe and decides against ironing it, because what's the point with this humidity? He takes his old working shirt off, leaves it hanging from a chair, puts the clean one on, and then looks at himself in the small mirror on the wall. He gets the comb out from the back pocket of his jeans, tries to flatten the fluffy mess on the top while he thinks once again that besides cars and cattle prods, there's still the humidity to worry about. But it'll rain, tonight it'll rain, the sky is rumbling like it's the end of the world. It'll rain — he can feel it in his bones. Everything will flood, people will be crushed by falling trees, or drown sucked in by manholes. And yet tomorrow will be better.

He grabs an umbrella from the stand and leaves, unaware that no one will ever collect that red paper from his desk after the summer break. The student's name rings a bell. But then, all names feel familiar when you live off memories.

A SENSE OF IMPENDING DOOM

"The only solution to all of this is a theocracy," he says, searching for my face in the rearview mirror. I'm at odds with this observation, but I nod in agreement anyway. Right now, I'd very likely answer nodding in agreement to any claim, no matter how mad, anything to avoid exchanging opinions with a stranger. "Do you know what a theocracy is?" he asks, his little eyes again in the rearview mirror, those incautious eyes so eager to rest on mine, those eyes that should be watching the road. I'm about to surrender to his eagerness for conversation, and admit I don't know what he means by "theocracy", so that he can spell it out for me, but he starts speaking before I've had a chance: "it's the government of the people, by God — that's a theocracy. And a theocracy is the only thing that can sort out all of this mess." When he says "all of this mess", he takes his right hand off the steering wheel and makes an all-encompassing gesture to indicate "everything".

"That's interesting," I say, wishing I had a book, a newspaper, anything to pretend that I'm busy or distracted.

But the only thing I can do to escape his verbal chokehold is to look out of the window.

The world outside comes at me as a succession of flat houses and the occasional ugly building in need of maintenance, cars that backdate a few decades, horse-drawn carts full of junk and cardboard, school children with once white aprons, people hiding from the sun under newspapers, broken pipes flooding the sidewalks, and dry squares that make you thirsty just looking at them, and that could very well use the water from the broken pipes. I don't like what I see. And yet, I refuse to agree with him. Perhaps the best thing to do would be to close my eyes; but I don't do that, because we're stopping at some traffic lights, and one always has to be vigilant when the car isn't moving. A man begging with a rusty tin comes to my window. He's covered in sweat and I can smell him from inside the taxi, even with the strong perfume that emanates from the air freshener — a green flat pine hanging from the rearview mirror. I wave him away, apologising for not having any change. He curses me and walks back to the sidewalk, dragging his crooked right foot on the concrete. His face betrays the pain that the whole operation involves.

"Never give them any money! If I can drive this, so can he!" says the taxi driver.

"I'm not sure he can drive with that foot..." I say.

"It's all play-acting! They've brought all these fake cripples from the ex-Yugoslavia. They brought them after the war," he says.

"Who did?"

"The government!"

"I see..."

A FOREIGN COUNTRY IS THE PAST

"Yes. The other night I was having a break in a bar downtown and there was one of these crooks begging from the cars that stopped at the traffic lights. He'd limp and beg when the cars were there, but when the lights turned green, and the cars were gone, he'd walk to a doorway floating like a ballerina, sit down, light a cigarette and relax. And imported cigarettes too! I'm telling you — it's all play-acting. They must make more money than you and me together. I wish I could get into this begging grift, to be honest, because with this taxi I'm not getting any richer." The lights change and he speeds ahead. "Do you go to church often?" he asks, eyes in the mirror again, those tiny black eyes in the mirror, just above the air freshener, searching for mine.

"It's been a while," I say. Quite a while. Probably five or six years. That time it wasn't an emergency — I went to someone's baptism. Or was it communion? I can't remember.

"Life gets in the way, I guess," he says. "And then you get overcome by a sense of impending doom and you end up running to the biggest church you can find. Right?" he says.

"Indeed," I say. I'm about to ask how he could tell I'm overcome by a sense of impending doom, but then it hits me — the only way I could look more like someone gripped by it would be if I carved OVERCOME BY A SENSE OF IMPENDING DOOM on my forehead. "Yes, I'm properly overcome by a sense of impending doom today, sir," I concede.

"Well, son. This too shall pass," he offers. "Sit in there for a while, have a word with the Bearded Guy, and things will get better. Then try to attend mass more regularly, get ready for the theocracy that's coming. Because it's coming and you want to be in the good books. You want to be in the good books, I'm telling you..." Here the taxi climbs up the road that leads to the cathedral, and soon it stops opposite the entrance. I give him enough money to pay for what's flashing on the clock and tell him to keep the change. I get out.

"Send my greetings!" he shouts and drives off before I've had time to reply.

It has to be said, the Cathedral has changed quite a bit since they privatised it a couple of years ago. In a good sense: it's been done up and it's cleaner, even considering the smell of burning wax, myrrh, rotten flowers, and damp wood that slaps you on the face as soon as you walk in. There's even a suited concierge welcoming people as they walk through the door. His desk is by the stoup where you wash sin off your hands, which now also acts as a water dispenser. I pour myself a glass of chilled Holy Water, drink it, toss the plastic cup in the bin, and then walk over to the concierge.

"Good afternoon. How can we help you?" he says.

"Hi, good afternoon. I'm here because I'm overcome by a sense of impending doom and I need to have a word with someone," I say.

"Sorry to hear that you aren't feeling very well. Do you have an appointment?"

"I'm afraid that I don't," I say. "I started to feel overcome by a sense of impending doom after lunch, after a call bearing what could be bad news," I explain, apologetically and perhaps unnecessarily.

"Not to worry. I'll see what we can do," he says, checking on his computer. "Right... We might be able to squeeze you between the two forty-five and the three p.m. appointments," he says.

"That's fantastic. Much appreciated. Who's seeing today?"

"Today's the Holy Spirit."

"I see..." — I fail to hide my disappointment.

"Yes, the Father sees on Thursdays and Fridays, and the Son sees over the weekend this time of the year, until Easter. I still have some slots for any of them, if you wish to return another time..." he adds, seizing the opportunity to try to get rid of me.

"No, it's fine! The Holy Spirit will be perfect!"

"Right then... Sure... I need to run some questions past you, if you don't mind..." he says, pressing the return key on his keyboard a few times.

"Please go ahead."

"I take it you are a Catholic," he says, raising his eyes and looking at me over his glasses.

"I am, yes. Sacraments and all."

"Do you come to church regularly?"

"Not regularly, I'm afraid, no."

"Are you overcome by a sense of impending doom often?"

"First time it's happened, but I suspect it'll happen more often from now on."

"Don't worry: we'll get to the bottom of it."

"That would be great."

"When was the last time you came to church?"

"A baptism or a communion a while back. About six years ago. I can't remember very well..."

"That's fine. It's just to have a better idea of your habits… Do you sin often?"

"Quite often."

"What kind of sins?"

"The usual stuff for a guy my age. But nothing serious. No killing, or stealing, or anything terrible like that."

"Good, good, always good to hear that." He types for a few moments on his keyboard, presses the return button a few more times. "Right… That's all. Now go and take a seat in the waiting room. We'll let you know when your time comes… I mean, not *that time*!" he jokes.

"Ha! Thanks a lot," I say and walk into the room next door.

You could very easily confuse this place for a dentist's waiting room, were it not for all the religious iconography hanging from the walls. The Virgin, Jesus Christ nailed to the cross, the Holy Spirit, saints undergoing torture, the usual stuff. And as you would expect, almost everyone here is old. There are six women who must be in their seventies, and the only other young person besides me is a chap who can't be more than sixteen or seventeen, who looks even more overcome by a sense of impending doom than I. Curiously, none of the old women seem overcome by a sense of impending doom — that kind of blasé attitude to life must come with age.

I head to the rightmost corner, where there's an empty chair, and sit next to one of the old women, this one Mumbling a prayer with rosary beads in her right hand. She moves to the side to make room for me, even though she didn't need to.

"Thanks," I say. She doesn't respond but smiles at me and keeps Mumbling.

There's a magazine rack to my left. I grab a copy of a weekly that specialises in celebrity news, and enter a world of young people in swimsuits by a pool or at the seaside, socialites at parties, a popular politician showing off his summer home with his family and four labradors, this or that partially naked model selling this or that product — a priest walks into the waiting room and calls a name. One of the old women — one at the opposite end, but she could be any of them — gets up and walks out.

"I'm here because my son can't find a job," says the old woman sitting next to me.

"Oh, I see!" I say. "I thought that was covered by Saint Cajetan," I add.

"These days, everything is more flexible. You can just pretty much go anywhere and they'll see you," she says.

"Yes, quite a good service," I say.

"So much better than before," she says, and then falls silent, staring at me with vacant eyes. Not really silent, because she keeps whispering her prayer, rolling the beads in her right hand. She isn't really staring at me either, she's more like in a trance. Soon she closes her eyes and turns her head to face the front.

I wonder if all these old women come here to discuss other people's problems, and for that reason, they aren't overcome by a sense of impending doom about themselves? Maybe. The lad, on the other hand, looks more overcome by a sense of impending doom by the minute. What has happened to him, I wonder — it must be something terrible. Suddenly, as if my thoughts had stirred him, he gets up, comes closer and stops by the magazine rack and shuffles through it, until he finds a copy of one of the Sunday papers' football supplements. Then he heads back to his seat. He could have grabbed any other magazine, because he just turns the pages without even looking at them. I feel a bit guilty about the thought, but I'm actually glad I'm not as overcome by a sense of impending doom as he is. Because this might mean that things will be OK, that the feeling of oppression in my chest will recede by itself, like a fever, and that everything will return to normal sooner or later. I go back to my magazine and start reading an article about a new TV show where unsuspecting people are filmed with hidden cameras as actors make their lives hell. The article describes how this sixty-seven-year-old man had his Ford Falcon — which was up for sale outside of his house — crushed by an army tank. In the end the production ended up paying four times the asking price, so the man was very happy, even if he had a minor heart attack. The TV of the future will consist mainly of shows like this, the article says.

Now the old woman who went in a few minutes ago walks back into the waiting room and then out to the main hall, and I guess the exit. I didn't have a chance to look at her face but for some reason, I believe she might have been crying. The problem is that when you are overcome by a sense of impending doom, you think everyone is having a terrible time too. Maybe she was OK. Maybe those spasms meant she was overcome with ecstasy. Maybe she was laughing. Who am I to say? They should make projecting things onto others a sin — if not one of the serious ones, at least a cardinal one like gluttony or sloth.

A FOREIGN COUNTRY IS THE PAST

After a while it's just the lad and me in the waiting room — they've must have stopped taking people in without an appointment by now. One thing that they could really do to improve the service even more is extending the opening hours. Or at least they could set up a hotline you can call, like some of the other once publicly-owned companies have been doing: the telephone, gas, electricity, and water suppliers, the train companies and so on. Some even shut down all their offices and *see you* only over the phone. Obviously old people like to do things in-person and can't get their head around doing anything over the phone, but I sincerely wouldn't mind just calling a number from the comfort of my home. Not that you need to be face to face with God to be face to face with God. At the end of the day, He's everywhere. You could be talking to a wall and you'd still be talking to God.

"Got the time, boss?" asks the lad. I check my watch.

"It's twenty past three."

"Thanks," he says, with a tone that signals annoyance, which I guess is an improvement from being overcome by a sense of impending doom.

"What time is your appointment?" I ask.

"Three p.m. Problem is a lot of people just turn up without an appointment and they always end up running late... What time is yours?"

"Quarter to three," I lie.

"Oh, that sucks."

"I've got nothing else to do," I say and go back to my magazine, retreating in guilt for lying to him, in a church of all places.

"How long have you been overcome by a sense of impending doom?" he asks, trying to keep me talking.

"Oh, well, since lunchtime... Girlfriend bearing some bad news... What about you?"

"I don't have a girlfriend."

"I mean, how long have you been overcome by a sense of impending doom?"

"Ah, right! Couple of years?"

"Couple of years? That sucks, mate!"

"Yes. But it's getting better now."

"Been coming here long?"

"Half a year or so... Twice a week... Religiously."

"Well, I don't see how it could be otherwise!" I add, unable to resist. He misses the joke. "Always with the Holy Spirit?" I ask.

"Yes. Always with the Holy Spirit." We run out of words and just stare at each other in silence.

"It's the first time I've come in years. Hadn't been in since before the privatisation," I say, breaking the uncomfortable quiet spell.

"What do you think?" he asks.

"Yeah, well, looks good so far. They've done up the cathedral quite a bit."

"Much better. Used to be a shithole, said my dad. A bit pricey now but it's worth it."

"What do you mean pricey? Do you have to pay?"

"Of course you have to pay!"

"Oh, that sucks. I didn't bring cash or anything."

"Don't worry about that. They can make you a payment plan. Thirty, sixty, ninety days, low interest rates."

"That's great!" I say.

"They've thought it all, really."

"Sounds like they did."

"God is infinitely intelligent, innit?"

"He sure is," I say and we both nod in agreement a couple of times. Now our words have truly been depleted. I go back to my magazine. Miraculously or not, the page I'm holding open has an advert for a store that sells home appliances. All of their products are also offered for thirty, sixty, or ninety days, with zero interest rate. I close the magazine. "You know, I never understood this Holy Spirit thing," I say. The lad looks around, as if concerned someone could be listening.

"What don't you understand?"

"What He's supposed to be."

"Well, He's like a dove, right? I mean, He isn't a dove, but looks like one, right?"

"Yeah, I know that. But what is He supposed to be? I get God and Jesus but I don't get the Holy Spirit," I explain.

"Well, at the end of the day, They're all the same thing, aren't They?" he says.

"Yeah, They're all the same but They really aren't."

"The Holy Spirit is sort of like the fuel of God… Maybe?"

"I've got no idea. That doesn't sound right tho…"

"Well, I don't know… You should probably ask the Holy Spirit when you get in," he says, going back to his magazine.

"I probably should," I answer but he's no longer listening. I'm pretty sure we studied the Holy Ghost in Catechism with Father Aldo but I can't remember exactly what the deal was with Him. And is it a He? Can a spirit ever be a He? Can a dove be a He? The priest who came before to fetch the old lady walks into the room and calls me in.

The Holy Spirit is on a desk, pecking at some birdseed. He or She or It looks like a dove, which as my earlier companion said, doesn't imply He or She or It actually is one. There's nothing special about He or She or It — He or She or It looks like a regular, run-of-the-mill dove. When I walked into the room, the Holy Spirit turned His or Her or Its head to inspect me better. Even in this, He or She or It acts like a normal dove. He or She or It is now looking at me with His or Her or Its left eye.

"Have a seat, please," the Holy Spirit says.

"Sure. Thanks for seeing me without an appointment."

"My pleasure. Right... Let's go over this quickly. I've been looking at your file and I see that you are currently overcome by a sense of impending doom. Correct?"

"Yes, correct."

"And this is because you have received a concerning phone call from your girlfriend. Correct?"

"Yes, that's correct."

"Her period is several weeks late. Correct?"

"Correct. Three weeks late. But I didn't tell the receptionist that."

"I know you didn't. I'm the Holy Spirit," He or She or It explains.

"Yes, of course! How silly of me!"

"No need to beat yourself up..."

"So what can I do about all this?"

"Well, the first thing to know is that there's no need to worry about it because tomorrow, by the Grace of God, the concern will be over, since your girlfriend will receive her period, also by the Grace of God, in the early hours of the morning. Amen," He or She or It says, giving me the left eye.

A FOREIGN COUNTRY IS THE PAST

"Amen!" I say, and I'm so happy, I could hug Him or Her or It, but since I've never hugged a dove before, I quickly dismiss the idea. I feel like a huge weight has been taken off my shoulders, and I stop being overcome by a sense of impending doom there and then.

"Now, thinking long term, you will need to refrain from activities that can cause you this kind of anxiety. Correct?"

"Yes, I know. I agree with that."

"You must be aware that we have a very clear code of conduct that determines whether you are a good Catholic or not."

"Yes, I'm aware. And I apologise for any transgression. How many Hail Marys do I get for this?"

"This doesn't work like that any more!"

"It doesn't?"

"No. You get additional interest rate points now."

"Oh!"

"Still, as this is your first time here with this kind of predicament, I'll wave the penalty points away."

"That's very kind of you!"

"Anything else you want to discuss? Otherwise I need to keep seeing these people before they go and convert to those evangelicals around the corner," He or She or It says.

"No, nothing really. Actually… How do I pay?"

"We'll send you an invoice. Then you can set up a payment plan if you need to."

"Do you need my address? Of course you don't!" I say. The Holy Spirit moves to stare at me with His or Her or Its other eye now.

"Anything else?" He or She or It says.

I ponder for a minute whether I should ask Him or Her

or It what's the deal with this dove thing. But instead of doing that I say "thank you", get up, and leave.

Before I step through the door, I can hear Him, Her or It cooing behind me.

I sit on a bench in the shade, in the square opposite the cathedral. It's full of pigeons and I wonder if one of them is the Holy Spirit of another religion, a religion no one has ever heard about. They peck at the ground, walk moving their heads like pigeons, coo like pigeons, eventually fly away like pigeons, to be replaced by other pigeons that look like pigeons. The pigeons soon get boring and I look at the passersby: men carrying briefcases, women in miniskirts and heels, truants with loosened ties, barefoot street urchins, a couple of guys dressed in sailor uniforms, all of them struggling in the heat — all of them ignore the pigeons, no time for mystical questions as they suffer under the sun. There's also a blind man begging on the cathedral steps. He lifts a rusty tin every time he hears someone walk up. Every other person throws some coins in his tin, every now and then someone dumps a folded note — each time he bows to thank them. After ten or twelve churchgoers give him money, he folds his white cane, removes his glasses and walks into the cathedral. A miracle or a grifter, I don't know. And here I remember the taxi driver from earlier. The thought of him spouting mad theories in his air-conditioned car fills me with joy — I can't say why exactly, but it fills me with joy. Perhaps I've been touched by the grace of God.

I stay in the shade a while longer, pondering whether I should call my girlfriend to break the good news. But since she's Jewish, I feel the good news will get lost in translation, that I'll spend a long time trying to explain the thing about the dove that isn't a dove, and how it doesn't really matter what the dove is, since God, Jesus and the Holy Spirit are actually the same guy — all that talking for nothing. Also, she's at work until seven and won't be able to take my call. This gives me three hours to kill. Maybe I should go to the river terminal and take a boat to the island, escape the city heat and spend the afternoon there, drinking cold beer in one of the shacks on the beach. Or maybe I could just go back into the cathedral, sit down for a while, and enjoy the air conditioning until they close for the day. By then the heat should have receded a bit. And if it hasn't, may God help us all.

TILES, TRACES OF FORMER ROOMS, PIPES

There's a large group of people blocking the pavement that leads to the bank. I should have settled the bills yesterday, or I should have come after lunch. Today pensioners get paid and they always turn up en masse in the morning, to dodge the midday sun. But even being payday, something doesn't look right. Yes, it's mainly old folk here, but there's something about the way they behave that doesn't fit with what you'd expect of a bank queue. For example, they aren't waiting in line, and instead they're all gathered in an amorphous noisy cluster that seems about to spill over into the road and the front gardens of the neighbouring houses. It looks more like a mob than a queue, an impression intensified by the way they bang pots and pans and set stuff on fire.

I manage just a couple of steps into this frenzied human mass, when I lose my bearings and I stop. Old men, old women, some in tears, all of them furious. I'm about to make sense of their prosthodontic glossolalia when I catch

Armilla's eyes just a couple of metres away — she's stuck just like me. We exchange tepid smiles and ceremonial nods and start pushing towards one another, attracted like two trains on a collision course, but gently pushing pensioners to the sides as we advance, instead of running them over as a train would.

"Hey!" she says, when we finally meet and exchange kisses that fail to land on our cheeks.

"How are you doing?" I ask.

"I'm doing well, all things considered," she says. "How are you doing?"

"I'm doing well too," I say. "What's going on here?"

"Haven't you heard?"

"No. I was about to make sense of what they're saying when I spotted you, and was suddenly overwhelmed by your presence and couldn't hear anything any more."

"I hate it when that happens," she says.

"Does it happen to you too?" I ask.

"No, I mean I hate it when you zone out."

"I know you do. So, what's going on?" I insist, avoiding her unsubtle attack.

"The bank's gone," she says.

"What?" I ask, feigning surprise out of politeness, as it isn't the first time this has happened since things started to go downhill a few months ago.

"What you've heard! Gone! There's nothing left... Even the building's gone," says Armilla, now pointing with her long right index finger to the place where until yesterday was the bank. I rise on my tiptoes to get a better view. Yes, gone — none of the three storeys are there any more. It's as if someone had used a massive cake knife to cut the bank out of the block. Or perhaps a cut isn't the right way to describe what has happened here, because this is no clean incision: there are tiles, the traces of former rooms, pipes, even a poster for a new savings account, still visible on the walls of the neighbouring buildings.

"Oh, this is bad!" I say.

"You can say that again!" says Armilla. "I needed to pay my bills."

"Same here," I say. "And they're due today!"

"I know!" she says.

"Now they'll cut my supply," I say.

"And mine! And in this weather!" she offers.

"Yes, that makes it much worse," I agree. "And not to mention all my savings are gone…" I add, deflated.

"Same here…" she says, deflated too. "I should have stashed my money under the mattress. At least thieves have the decency to leave the building intact most of the time."

"It sucks to live like this…" I reflect aloud, and we both fall silent.

The silence extends for a ridiculous amount of time. The next thing I know is that we're alone, standing in the middle of the pavement, next to a pile of burning tyres and two toppled cars, a plume of black smoke climbing up in the air. Everyone's gone and the sun stings, so we must have been staring at each other in silence for a couple of hours or more. And when I'm able to speak again, I do it saying something I know I'll regret. "So… do you want to go somewhere with aircon to grab a coffee and catch up?"

"I don't think we should," she says, and I sigh with relief. And maybe because I sigh so loudly she adds, "But let's go anyway. There's that nice café round here... You know the one where we used to go—"

"Yes, yes, I know which one," I interrupt. What a cheap shot picking that café, of all the cafés in the world. "Are you sure it's still there?" I ask.

"Well, when the cafés start going like the banks, then we'll know we've got a very serious problem," she says. I don't know what she means, because I'd much rather the café had gone instead of the bank with my money.

"OK, let's go then," I surrender.

We walk in silence under the scorching sun. One in two shops looks permanently closed, and the ones that are open are completely void of customers. There are young kids begging from door to door, but no one seems to answer their calls. Opposite the supermarket entrance, a group of police officers stand aimlessly and smoke, covered in sweat, telling each other jokes. We walk past an elderly couple living in a tent; she heats up a rusty kettle on a small fire, while he reads the paper; one of their dogs can't stop scratching, and the other one licks its balls. We walk past another bank that's also gone - in its place only angry people and a hole remain. And those tiles, the traces of former rooms, pipes, and posters for new saving accounts, of course. It's sad to behold, it can't be anything but sad. But what bothers me the most, much more than all of this banking nonsense, the state of it all, the unemployment, the food raids that can't be too far away as December gets hotter by the minute, the thousands choosing exile by the day, is that I know very well what will happen now with Armilla. I know we'll sit at the same table we used to sit at, chat amicably for half an hour, talk about how bad this summer is turning out to be and how horrible things are right now, pretend that we can be friends, and then we'll bump into a minor disagreement — something truly microscopic — and our conversation will grow more and more tense, until we end up shouting how much we hate one other in front of terrified punters and the café staff. And then I'll rest my hand on top of hers, say that I'm sorry, that I didn't want things to end the way they did, that it was all my fault, it's always my fault. And she'll say she didn't want things to end that way either and yes, I'm right, it was my fault, it always is. And we'll kiss and we'll go to her place, have great sex in her muggy bedroom, end up covered in sweat and other body fluids, and everything will start again, all the mad fucking will start again, and all the fighting will start again, because I can't stay quiet under pressure, with the added inconvenience of having no electricity, gas, water, nor savings, because my bank, our bank, is gone. And who knows what will be gone next.

"What are you thinking about?" she asks. "You're very quiet."

"I was thinking about those tiles."

"Which tiles?"

"D'you know when a building is gone and you can still see the old tiles? I mean the toilet or kitchen tiles, on the walls of the buildings that remain around the empty space... Know what I mean? The tiles... The traces of former rooms, the pipes sticking out, all of that... There were some of these tiles on the walls of the buildings that used to surround our bank."

"And what's with that?"

"Seeing those leftovers made me very sad," I explain.

She doesn't reply at first. Instead she gets her cigarettes out and stops to light one. She offers me her pack and lighter, and I get a cigarette and light up too.

"You say the stupidest things sometimes," she says. She blows smoke on my face and then keeps walking.

And she's right, I do say the stupidest things sometimes, I think, as I jog to catch up with her, telling myself that things can always get worse, but hoping that things will be better this time.

WHEN THINGS WERE GOOD

One by one the shops closed down, leaving just their watch repair store at the back and the bar — a small kiosk with four or five stools near the entrance. It was the same all over the old city centre, with arcades being replaced by blocks of flats and parking lots. It was sad and you can't resist change forever, but you can't surrender to it without a fight either — that had been their reasoning, and that's why they had rejected the developers' offer.

When things were good, Irene would arrive at the arcade every morning around quarter to eight, grab a coffee from the bar, open up, and get ready to receive the jobs at eight. Then, while she waited for the first customers to come in, she'd get lost in admin — things like faxing the providers to order imported pieces from the capital, keeping the books up to date, paying the bills, anything that didn't require staring into watches with a monocle whilst trying to replace a cog. The repairs were Chobi's domain. He'd arrive an hour after her and start operating on the watches and clocks, which could be dozens at a time, all ticking at their own tempo on his worktable. They'd work until one, go back home just a few blocks away, have lunch, take a short nap, then come back to open again at four, work until seven-thirty or eight depending on the day, and maybe end their shift sharing a beer at the bar with some of the other shop owners. Much like with the ticking of a clock, there was a certain rhythm to this routine — a rhythm that had remained the same in its basic aspects for a very long time. They had started young and childless, and thirty years later, still childless, they had learned to love the reassuring repetition of minor tasks together, often in silence, surrounded by the hypnotic music of clocks and watches. Like this, without much effort of the imagination, but with plenty of hard work and patience, they had lived a pleasant life, with a relatively regular income.

That was when things were good. Now that things weren't good at all, they might as well have stayed closed, and maybe it was indeed time to sell or rent the premises out, if someone would want to open a shop in a dying arcade. But they kept opening anyway, out of habit. Only that she'd stay at the bar drinking coffee and reading the paper or a book, and head to the shop when she saw someone going in, something that happened less and less. Soon Chobi stopped coming unless there was a job to fulfil; until he stopped coming at all. At some point, the ticking music was almost imperceptible in the shop, kept by four or five repairs that had never been collected.

Now Irene is sitting on one of the bar stools, reading the newspaper's police section, pressing the paper against the bar to prevent its pages from fluttering away thanks to the draught generated by a noisy fan. Yesterday morning a pickpocket got killed by a mob three blocks away. He was chased off the bus by some of the passengers after he tried to rob an old woman, got caught before he disappeared in the crowd, was punched and kicked to death — a damning indictment of our society, when decent people take matters into their own hands, says the anonymous writer.

"That was opposite the bank," says Fabre, the bar owner, peering at the paper, pointing with his head as if Irene could have any doubts he's talking about the pickpocket.

"Yes, I've read it. Terrible!"

"I was there when it happened," says Fabre.

"In the bank?"

"There in the street! I was on my way here when they caught him. I saw everything!"

"Oh!" says Irene. "That has to be horrible to watch!"

"Not really... He had it coming," says Fabre.

"I guess so. But still..."

"Still what?"

"We can't just kill people when they steal a wallet, can we?"

"We should," says Fabre, opening a drawer and showing Irene a pistol without taking it fully out. "We should, because these crooks never learn. People are fed up with getting robbed," he adds and closes the drawer.

Irene doesn't reply and an uncomfortable silence ensues. Luckily the bar telephone rings and Fabre heads to the back to answer.

When things were good, there was a perfume store, a nappy shop, a suitcase repair shop, a travel agency, a cobbler, a stamp maker, a tie shop, a record shop, the bar, and their watch repair shop. The first one to go was the suitcase repair shop, which must have been a front for something, because no one ever walked in with broken suitcases, and yet people were still leaving with them, which made no sense at all. Then the perfume shop went, followed by the nappy place, and then the stamp maker. When and in what order the other ones went bust, Irene can't recall very well. But she's pretty sure the tie shop closed down just before the new government took over. She remembers this because she thought "what a pity they're closing, now that things will finally get better and men will need ties for their job interviews."

But things never got better — they just got different.

Irene sinks her lips in the coffee cup while she watches Fabre move behind the bar — he's pushing mugs and plates around, occasionally grabbing a dirty piece of cloth to wipe some area of the bar, making it even dirtier. Fabre is a big man, not fat but big and in many ways he reminds her of her father. He was a good man, her father, a gentle giant. Big men tend to be nice. Fabre might be an exception, if he thinks it's OK to kill people over a wallet. He must feel her gaze on him, because he stares back and their eyes meet briefly. Then he walks towards her, carrying a pile of takeaway cups and what looks like a box of sugar sticks.

"It's quiet," he says.
"Yes, very quiet."
"The weather doesn't help."

"No, it never helps when it's hot like this."

"Not even takeaways from the lads that used to stop in the corner... A few of them still drop by to say hi when they drive past. But none today."

"Where do they stop now?"

"They're all at the new mall near the old train station. That's where all the taxis stop now. Anyway, I can't complain: the kid's still delivering some orders for me. So that's something."

"I never remember that kid's name but he seems decent," says Irene.

"Carlos. Yes, decent kid — he works hard and doesn't cost me much," says Fabre and then places the cups on the bar. "How's Chobi? I hardly ever see him any more," he says.

"No point him keep coming in, if there's nothing to do."

"Things are tough right now."

"Yes, they are. But it's more those disposable watches that they sell everywhere. Those Chinese watches. They are much cheaper than fixing a real one."

"You can't stop time," says Fabre.

"Well, if it stops, we can still fix it," says Irene and they both laugh. "Maybe that's what we really need — time to stop, until things are good again. Because if things stay this way, we might have to sell."

"That would be bad," says Fabre.

"Yes, it would be. But it is what it is," says Irene.

"I won't sell," says Fabre. "I know it's pissing them off but I won't sell."

"Who is it pissing off?"

"The developers who bought all the other shops. They

want to demolish the arcade, and build a block of flats. We're holding them back."

"Ah, yes, of course... But that isn't what they told us. When they offered to buy us out, they said they just wanted to build some flats on the upper floor, and revamp the arcade, give it a new lease of life."

"In any case, they need us to go."

"In any case, yes. Well, we won't sell."

"And I won't sell either. Unless, of course, they offer well above market value. Then I'll think about it."

"You have to do what you have to do, right?" says Irene, trying to end the pointless conversation. Her gaze drifts involuntarily to the drawer where Fabre keeps his gun. He catches her eyes again. She looks elsewhere but there isn't much to keep her attention, so she drifts back to the drawer.

"I've had it for years," says Fabre.

"Have you ever shot anyone?" asks Irene.

"That isn't something you should be asking!" says Fabre, smiling. Irene smiles back, even if she finds his answer very annoying. She won't ask him again, that's for sure.

"Can I have that paper again?" she says instead.

"It's not like anyone is dying to read it right now," says Fabre, tossing it on the bar.

Irene folds the paper in two and uses it to fan herself. Then she opens it again and continues reading the pickpocket article.

He was twenty years old, came from one of the slums, had a long police record, had served a couple of years for theft, followed one of the local teams everywhere, had a drug problem, no one would give him a job, so he had to steal, but he was always a good son, and he didn't deserve to die like a dog, his mother says. No arrests were made and his murder will be shelved with other murder cases; but before this happens, the police chief is quoted begging people not to act violent, even against parasitic thieves, that these are hard times but we still have Christian values and a duty to treat others as human beings, and he implores that witnesses come forward. Obviously no one will come forward; no one ever does, because doing so would mean breaking with the unspoken agreement that some people do deserve to die like dogs. Surely the police chief knows this, but he has to say what he has to say. You have to do what you have to do.

By the time she's done with the article, she doesn't remember the pickpocket's name any more. It isn't even the only homicide in the police section. She pushes the paper away from her on the bar, as if in that way she could take a distance from it all. She returns to the shop while Fabre is at the back of the kiosk, torturing a blender.

She's reading her book, an incredibly boring romantic novel that takes place in Siberia in the nineteenth century, when she hears the bangs outside. Two blasts, pretty much like firecrackers, one after the other. But it's too early for Christmas, or rather too late, since it's January, and there's no such a thing as a kid saving firecrackers for later. "Fabre must have shot someone," is the most rational explanation her brain comes up with. She cracks open the door and peeks outside and everything looks as usual. But a hot breeze brings in the smell of gunpowder.

From where she's standing, she can only see the back of the kiosk, no windows this side. The wise thing to do would be to lock herself in and call the police and let them do their work, but curiosity gets the best of her and she leaves the shop and starts to move slowly towards the bar, creeping along the vacant windows, ready to jump back inside if needed. She treads carefully, doing her best not to let her knees or ankles click. She stops by the door of what used to be the suitcase repair shop, to scan for the smallest of noises — there's a little parapet dividing the empty units that she can use to hide and listen better. But she can't hear anything. Carlos finds her like this — half-crouched behind the parapet — when he walks into the gallery, rolling his tray in the air and catching it with both hands before it falls.

"Hey Mrs Irene! All good?" he greets her.

"Hi! Yes, all good! Been out delivering coffees?" says Irene, straightening up and trying to look casual.

"Yes! How did you guess?"

"The tray..." says Irene.

"Yes, of course!" says Carlos.

"Carlos! The drinks are getting cold!" shouts Fabre from inside the kiosk.

"Coming!" answers Carlos. He winks at Irene and walks into the bar.

Irene walks towards the arcade's exit. Once her eyes get used to the brightness, she looks both ways: the smell of gunpowder lingers in the air but there is nothing out of the ordinary — just people passing by, looking hot on

A FOREIGN COUNTRY IS THE PAST

the pavement, looking hot in cars, looking hot on the bus, looking hot on bikes. She heads back inside and stops at the bar. Now it takes some moments for her eyes to get used to the dark. Fabre is whipping the counter, as usual; Carlos is loading his tray to go out on another round.

"Heard that just now?" she asks Fabre.

"Heard what?" he says.

"Those two bangs."

"No, I didn't hear anything."

"I didn't hear anything either," says Carlos and both Fabre and Irene look at him, as if they weren't expecting him to speak. "Sorry," he says and walks away carrying his tray full of takeaway cups.

"How strange. I swear I heard two bangs… They sounded like firecrackers — I can even smell the powder."

"Must have been the exhaust of a passing car," says Fabre.

"Yes, maybe it was that," says Irene.

She walks back to her shop, unconvinced by Fabre's explanation but pretty sure the bangs weren't a product of her imagination.

The rest of the morning drags on slowly, giving her a lot of time to think about the blasts. Eventually the mystery gets old and she lets it go and goes back to her book, which hasn't stopped being boring. She reads two pages, closes it, and to keep herself busy, she starts tidying up Chobi's tools, which are gathering dust on his table. He'd normally go crazy if she touched his tools without his permission, but right now he cares so little that she could very well bin them. She puts this thing here, this thing there, this other thing over there, pretty much at random. Eventually the table is empty and she has nothing else to do. Just at this moment, luckily, a man walks into the shop, not to order a repair but to ask if she knows where the suitcase people have moved to. He's a young man, possibly in his mid twenties. He doesn't carry a suitcase with him, nor does he look like the kind of person who'd own one, which confirms to Irene that the suitcase repair shop was a front, who knows what for. She sends him away, politely but with a moderate sense of disgust for whatever he's up to. Maybe it's time to go back home but she doesn't want to walk in the sun, not yet. So she sits and stares at a clock on the wall, literally, to make time.

Eventually she summons the courage and sets out to walk the few blocks to her flat, chasing whichever shade she can find. There aren't many trees in the city centre, and the ones there are rickety sticks unable to filter the midday sun. Everyone walks faster in the heat — it should be the opposite but everyone is in a rush to get somewhere cool. The only one who seems unfazed by it all is a cardboard picker, dragging his loaded cart in the middle of the road, followed by a long line of cars. He's wearing flip-flops and is dressed in rags. He's covered in sweat and bent forward, plodding along like a snail. The drivers behind him must be stunned because no one is honking the horn or shouting at him to hurry up.

When she arrives at exactly one-fifteen, Chobi is cooking steaks. Anyone walking past their flat at ground level would be able to tell that someone is cooking steaks in the building (and their flat is on a fifth floor). She can smell the steaks when she's getting in, she can smell them while she's throwing the key on the main door, she can smell them while she waits for the lift, then she can smell them as she travels in the airless lift, and she can definitely smell them in the fifth floor hallway. The smoke slaps her on the face as soon as she gets in the flat — it's a greasy mist that bewilders the senses, even with all the windows open and the timid breeze that gets in. She hates it when he cooks meat in the kitchen; she's told him a million times he should use one of the communal grills in the terrace for that. Just wait for the weekend and cook the meat then, like everyone else. Not that he even needs to wait for the weekend, since he's got nothing to do during the week.

At least he's had the decency of closing the bedroom door this time. She opens the door, gets in, shuts the door behind her, throws her handbag on a chair and lies in bed. She stares at the ceiling, spots the damp stains from when the flat upstairs had a leak, jumps on her feet and gets changed into something more comfortable, because those stains still make her blood boil. When she steps into the kitchen some minutes later, Chobi is sitting at the table, already halfway through his steak. The telly is on somewhere in the greasy mist.

"Hello there!" he says, happy to see her. "I've left you a steak on the skillet."

"I could smell the steak all the way from the shop," she says. "You know... Anyway, forget it." Irene walks to the stove, serves herself the steak on a plate, then heads to the table and takes the empty chair.

"Did you hear about the pickpocket? They've been on and on about it all day long," he says, nodding towards the screen. A man in a blue police uniform is talking to a reporter. At one point they cut to an image of a police van parked opposite the bank, and then the usual white and blue tape in the corner. Then they cut back to the officer and his generous moustache — he must be the same police chief who was quoted pleading for witnesses in the paper, since only a police chief could don such a moustache.

"Yes, I read it in the paper this morning."

"People are fed up," says Chobi. "People are tired of getting robbed. By politicians and by common crooks. They've had enough."

"You sound like Fabre."

"What's with Fabre?"

"He was there yesterday, when they killed him. He saw everything."

"Sure he did!"

"That's what he said."

"Bullshit."

"Why would he make it up?"

"Because he's a compulsive liar! Mention Columbus and he'll claim he was there when he arrived."

"And he said that people are tired of getting robbed and that the pickpocket deserved it."

"Well... What's the saying? Even a broken clock is right twice a day," Chobi says, suitably for a clockmaker.

Irene doesn't reply. She cuts a piece of meat, takes it to her mouth, bites through a nerve. She takes the half-chewed chunk of steak out of her mouth and places it on the plate.

"Then he showed me the gun he keeps in a drawer... What's more, he might have shot it in the arcade because

I heard two blasts... And when I came out of the shop it smelled like gunpowder," she says.

Chobi gazes at her in silence, wearing a serious expression. Then he bursts out laughing, so out of control that he almost chokes. It takes him about a minute to recover.

"He showed you his gun?" he says.

"Yes."

"And then he shot it in the arcade?" he adds and starts laughing again.

"Yes! Twice!"

"Irene: it's a toy gun!"

"It's a real gun!"

"It's a cap gun! He showed it to me too!"

"I know what a real gun looks like, Chobi!" shouts Irene, unable to contain her frustration.

"How would you know what a real gun looks like? Is there something that I need to know, Irene?"

"My dad owned guns! There were always guns in our house!"

"Did your father own a nine millimetre pistol?"

"What's that?"

"Fabre's toy!"

"There were revolvers in my house!"

"Listen, Irene: what Fabre showed you is a replica pistol. It's a cap gun — one of those Chinese toys they sell everywhere now. I've seen it. And it isn't even a good replica. If he tries to scare anyone with it, he'll get shot. Anyone can tell it's a toy gun!"

"Well, in my opinion, it does look real."

"No, it really doesn't."

"And what would *you* know?"

"I was conscripted, wasn't I?"

"That was so long ago you must have shot trebuchets," Irene says and both laugh.

They eat in silence, watching the news. She can't eat any more — she can't stand a nervy steak.

Chobi stays watching television and Irene goes back to the bedroom. She lays down and falls asleep immediately, even if it's unpleasantly hot, and she hasn't turned the fan or the air conditioning on. She wakes up covered in sweat an hour or so later. She feels like she might have been dreaming but she can't remember what she was dreaming about. She takes a quick cold shower, changes into a new dress. She leaves for the shop around three-thirty without saying goodbye to Chobi, who's laughing out loud in the kitchen, watching a talk show.

Outside it's still ridiculously hot. Things have a blurry edge around them, almost as if someone had rubbed them with the palm of their hand. The sun still falls like molten lead and there are few people about — only the crazy ones or those who have no choice but to leave their shelter. She's crossing the street when she steps on the liquefied tar that covers a pothole, and her right heel gets stuck. When she tries to move her foot, the heel snaps. She has to limp the four blocks to the arcade. When she arrives, in a bad mood, covered in sweat and dying to get a cold drink from the bar, she finds it closed. There's a sign taped to the door: "I'll be back soon. Fabre." Perhaps it's better he isn't here — perhaps it's better that he's somewhere else, showing off his stupid toy gun.

A FOREIGN COUNTRY IS THE PAST

She opens the shop door, gets in, and flips the sign, just out of habit. She turns the aircon on and soon it starts to get cooler. She remembers there's an old pair of flat shoes in the utility room and this brightens her mood. There's nothing to do so she starts reading her book again. Now the book isn't only boring, but the words stay with her for just two or three seconds, every phrase interrupted by the thought of a cold bottle of sparkling water. She puts the book down, grabs her bag, and leaves the shop again without turning off the aircon.

Now it feels even hotter but there is something pleasant about this oppressive feeling in her chest — perhaps it's just the promise of being back in the cool shop pretty soon, and with a cold drink. She walks fast under the sun, rushing to the bar in the other corner. When she's halfway through the block, she bumps into a man leaving a building. She almost ends up on the floor but he grabs her and steadies her.

"Sorry! My fault!" the young man says.

"No, it's my fault!" she answers.

"Are you OK?" he asks, politely.

"Yes, don't worry."

"Sorry again," he says and keeps walking.

His face rings a bell, but she can't say where from — maybe he's a former client. She continues the rest of her short journey and soon reaches the corner. The bar has air conditioning too and she feels her sweat getting colder as soon as she steps in. She shakes off the goosebumps and orders a bottle of sparkling water and an iced coffee. When she attempts to pay, she realises her bag is open and her wallet is missing. For a moment she wonders whether she could have dropped it in the shop or back home, but then she remembers the young man on the way to the bar and everything makes sense: his face was familiar because she bumped into the dead pickpocket. She stares blankly at the girl behind the bar.

"Are you OK?" the girl asks.

"I'm very sorry but my wallet is missing... I've just been robbed..." Irene says.

"Where?" the girl asks.

"On the way here!"

"But your shop is just on the other corner!"

"I know! And that isn't even the worst bit!"

"What else?"

"Oh, forget about it! You'll think I'm mad! And maybe I am... Let me go back home and get some cash for you."

"You can pay me tomorrow! Now go and report the theft to the police!"

"It's pointless! And I barely had any money."

"Still!"

"It's just a waste of time. A total waste of time... Anyway... Sure I can pay you tomorrow?"

"Sure."

"Thanks and sorry," Irene says and leaves.

She walks slowly back to her shop, literally dragging her flat shoes on the hot pavement. She should be angry but she's caught in a feeling she can't quite define. Is it sadness? Could she be feeling sad? Or is it impotence? Whatever it is, it isn't nice. It's the first time she's been robbed by someone who's dead, and it doesn't feel any better than when you get robbed by a living person. Maybe Fabre was right and these people never learn. But if they don't learn even in death, then what's to be done with them? It's a lose-lose situation, whichever way you see it.

When she arrives at the arcade, Fabre is opening the bar.

"God, what's got to you?" he says. "You look like you've seen a ghost." She just blanks him and walks into her shop.

Back inside, she pours the iced coffee in the sink and then heads to her desk. She rummages in the top drawer, until she finds the developer's card: MILIVIC CONTRACTORS, 341-409-3323. Persuading Chobi to sell won't be hard — clearly he's had enough. It'll be a pity to let the shop go, but sometimes you have to do what you have to do. And would it really be a pity to sell? Who's to say? Who's to say anything any more? Who's to say anything any more about anything at all?

SAINTS

Forget the two days of training, it was Zulma who told her everything she really needed to know about the job and it only took six words. "Remember: the client is the enemy," Zulma said on that first day, as Juli plugged the headset into the terminal for the first time.

At first, it was just that hoarse voice, coming from some spot in the mysterious aisle to her right. And then Zulma, who wasn't Zulma yet, who was just that hoarse voice, rolled back on her chair to reveal her human form. So now, there was also the large smile framed by red lips and stained teeth, the messy grey hair made messier by the misplaced headset, large bottle-bottom glasses, a long chain with a large crucifix resting over a bright red turtleneck sweater, a slightly deranged stare.

"I'm Zulma," she said.

"Nice to meet you. I'm Juli."

"Is that your real name or is it the one that came with the script? Because I've heard they're giving you all fake names now…"

"No, it's my real name."

"Work experience?"

"No, one year contract with possibility of renewal."

"I see... They never make it till the contract ends; and when they do, they don't get renewed... But anyway, I'm here if you need me," said Zulma.

"Thanks a lot."

"Just don't need me too often because I hate being interrupted when I'm on a call," said Zulma, and it was impossible to tell whether she was joking or not.

And that was enough socialising because there was a beep in her right ear and the first client barged in.

The calls start sharp at eight in the morning, because there's always a queue in the switchboard. They end at four in the afternoon, more or less, depending on when the last call comes in. The worst thing that can happen is getting a call just before four, with a complicated request. You still have to take it and resolve whatever needs resolving, and you have to do it for free. On the plus side, it doesn't count towards your average time.

There are two fifteen minutes breaks and a half hour lunch break that you can take whenever you want. Most people take a short break before noon, then have their lunch, then take another break a couple of hours later. You need to request these breaks in advance, and the system will authorise them when there are enough active operators. It isn't rare to have to wait for an hour or so for the break to be approved, which means you might end up taking most or all of them back-to-back, to avoid losing them.

There are two hundred and fifty operators in the day shift. Some of them work part-time, but the majority do the full eight hours. Most are young and straight out of school — on one year contracts like Juli, or doing a work experience. The older ones are all former employees from before the privatisation, who've been sent to the call centre so that they give up and quit, which is much cheaper than firing them.

The calls never stop coming in. When you finish with a caller there's a seven seconds' pause until the next one. So considering the breaks and the pace of the calls, most operators working full time take around one hundred and forty calls a day. Others — the really good ones — can take up to two hundred. If when you end the shift your average handling time is above three minutes, you get a point. If you get three points in one calendar month, you are out.

"You still look happy," said Zulma later that week, when they met in the kitchen during a break.

Juli said that she was happy, yes, because she hadn't been able to find a job for a very long time.

"You kids will never know what it's like to have a real job," said Zulma. "Working here is like working in that burger place they opened round the corner. The same thing but dealing with complaints instead of flipping burgers," she added.

"McDonald's?" said Juli.

"That one. That shithole is just like this one."

"Here it seems much better."

"Just give it time!"

"How long have you been here?"

"I can't even remember! More than twenty years, less than thirty."

"That's a long time!"

"That's a stupid time!" said Zulma. "Not always taking calls, though."

Zulma told her how things used to be much better when phones had rolling dials instead of keys, and how good her salary was back then, when the company was state-owned, when the union was strong, and there were great holiday camps the staff could go to on a budget, and other perks like that. Work wasn't bad either — at least it was more varied. Then things happened, she said, if you know what I mean, and Juli didn't know what Zulma meant, but she still nodded along to make it seem like she did. Zulma also said that she could hardly afford to pay her rent any more, and that she was trying to quit smoking to save money, but that the job didn't help. She said "I swear on this that this job doesn't help but I'm trying to quit," and kissed her crucifix. Juli — who had also noticed some holy cards with images of saints pinned to her cubicle — asked if she was religious. Zulma answered that she wasn't religious but spiritual. Then she lit a new cigarette with the one that was dying.

Now, almost a year later, Zulma has been on the line with the same client for over twenty minutes.

It's hard to say exactly what's going on — Juli has her own calls to worry about — but it seems Zulma's client is incredibly stubborn and passive-aggressive, and is keeping Zulma going in circles. The passive aggressive ones are the hardest to deal with, because you can't just end the call; it's much better when they lose it, swear at you, or threaten you, and you can hang up. After transferring a call about a faulty receiver to the technical team, Juli's attention drifts to Zulma.

"Sorry sir, but we've been over this already, for the past twenty-five minutes or so. I don't know how to explain it again. We can't do what you want — that isn't something we've got the power to do. Not me, nor any manager, and I can't transfer you to someone else for that simple reason. What you are asking for is technically impossible so—"

Then another beep on Juli's right ear as a new customer comes in. This time it's a woman asking for a payment plan for a large bill. This is the kind of call that can take well above the expected three minutes, so Juli focuses on her own business once again, and tries to do what needs to be done as fast as possible, because she was performing quite badly today, and this call has the potential to make everything even worse. She dives into the paperwork, taking bank details, identity numbers, specifying the amount of instalments to be paid, explaining to the woman what interest rates are and why they apply, then explaining to her that the practice is legal, that everyone adds a charge when offering a payment plan. Then she listens to the woman complain about interest rates, say that CommsTel are a bunch of money sharks, that things were better before, when it was state-owned, and you could go and talk to someone in person in the office, and you always ended up knowing the people who worked in customer service, and they were even nice and helpful, not just robots like now. Then Juli needs to ask for the bank details again because there's a number missing somewhere, and the woman can't find the paper from where minutes ago she read the wrong number to Juli; she gets nervous, ends up calling her son, who tells her that she's actually holding the paper. It takes three more attempts to get the number right. The next thing Juli knows about Zulma and her passive-aggressive client is a loud bang on her desk, which makes the cubicle walls shake. Juli pushes her chair backwards to look: Zulma is holding her temples. She presses the mute button, pulls from her hair, and brings her hands to her mouth.

"For the love of God, the Virgin and all the fucking Saints!" she shouts at a controlled volume, like all operators do when on the verge of bursting. A pink tsunami of blood starts climbing up the left side of her neck and soon the blush extends all the way up to her ears. She closes her eyes and clenches her teeth and bangs the desk two more times and the cubicle walls shake again.

Juli's about to mute herself to tell Zulma to take it easy and just hang up, but the old woman starts asking if she's still there and if the number is now right, and Juli goes back to the conversation. When she finishes the call, Zulma is still with the same customer — that's thirty-five minutes and counting. If Juli were handling that call, she'd probably lose it too. Her contract expires next week, and still there's no word on whether it'll be renewed or not.

People call for a variety of reasons. Faulty lines and technical problems, billing complaints, requests for new lines, new installations that are delayed (sometimes for years), lines that have been cut due to lack of payment; then there are kids who are bored and call to prank the operators, old lonely people who need to talk to someone and end up complaining about the most random of things, aspiring suicides who can't think of a better number to call. The best calls are the ones about technical issues, since these are forwarded to a technical team located elsewhere, and in a matter of seconds you're done. The worse kind of callers — even worse than the occasional suicide - are old people with billing complains. To the best of Juli's knowledge, they are always stubbornly wrong and simply forget the numbers they called. When the number they don't recognise belongs to a family member or friend, it's easy to get them to recant, but many times they simply can't remember calling a certain random number, and it takes the operators quite a while to convince them that the system is always right, that nothing can be done. Some lash out but the vast majority of them eventually give up and retreat in indignation. It's a waste of time for everyone involved, and it'd be better for everyone if they just refunded these calls, since we're talking about cents. But then it'd be a free-for-all, wouldn't it?

Some minutes later, when Juli is scaring a prankster by reading him the number he's calling from, she hears a very loud beep. It's definitely not the sound of the fire alarm — it isn't that loud, and it's a different tone, higher. She tells the kid that she'll have to report his parents to the police and he hangs up. She stands up and looks around. The operators from the other side of the aisle are also on their feet, trying to figure out where the sound is coming from.

It's coming from Zulma's computer terminal: she's hunched over like an idle ventriloquist dummy, her head slumped on the middle of the keyboard, pressing the keys, while on the computer screen a nonsensical script unfolds.

The first few days, Juli couldn't get the beeps that announce new calls out of her head. Beeps on the lift, beeps while waiting for the bus, beeps on the way home, beeps while taking a shower, beeps while having dinner, beeps while watching TV, beeps while trying to fall asleep. Each imaginary beep was an invitation to go over her script: "Good morning, my name is Juli. Thanks for calling CommsTel. How can I help you today?" The beeps even woke her up several times during the night. And a couple of times she actually started repeating her script aloud.

In the following weeks, the tinnitus joined in: a high frequency hissing sound that she could hear when it was quiet. Had this noise always been there and she hadn't realised? Or was it there because of the seven hours of wearing a headset five days a week? Then her first payslip arrived, and she decided the noise had always been there, and both the tinnitus and the beeps didn't bother her any more. It isn't that she stopped hearing them — it's just that she stopped caring. The money she'd get wasn't a fortune, but still, it was relatively good. And having a job right now, with things the way there were, was truly a miracle. Since she had dropped out of uni, she had applied to over thirty jobs with no luck. The jobs routinely involved selling mobile phones — mobile phones were all the rage but no one was making any money selling them, only the mobile phone companies. It was depressing to go to an interview and wait for hours for your turn, just to be told the job was on a commission-only basis, with no fixed salary. The interviewers always promised that she could earn a lot of money this way, but their cheap suits and tacky shoes told another story.

A FOREIGN COUNTRY IS THE PAST

Then her cousin Ciro—who works for HR at CommsTel—told her that there was an opening for several new positions in the call centre, that he would make sure she got in if she applied, that it wasn't that hard — she just needed to attend a recruitment event and pass a psychometric test. Ciro told her what to answer in the test. And when the interview came, he told her that she needed to appear trustworthy but not too ambitious, adaptable but not too clever, and that's what she did. She didn't even have to fake it. In some way she was destined for a career in the telecoms industry.

When it became clear that Zulma was dead, one of the supervisors covered her body with a promotional banner. She's still there, slumped on the desk under a white and blue CommsTell banner advertising a new combo for small businesses: landline and mobile phone, unlimited minutes, for a reasonable price, no installation costs. The computer stopped beeping at some point.

Everyone in her aisle got a one hour compassionate break on top of the regular ones, and now they are all sitting in the resting area, puffing away in silence, occasionally glancing at the partly-hidden corpse.

With her first wages, Juli bought a pair of running trainers for herself and a bottle of imported olive oil for her mother. She went shopping straight after work, almost running with excitement.

Later, when she was heading to the bus stop to hop on the bus home, she walked past the McDonald's they had recently opened round the corner from the call centre. There was a long queue that stretched all the way to the other end of the block. Most of the queuers were very young — the guys were dressed in suits, the girls in dresses that were too short. She felt sorry for them: flipping burgers for a living whilst wearing those silly hats must be hell. And she felt a sense of superiority that she hadn't felt before.

Then she took the bus home, making sure not to drop the olive oil, holding her handbag with both hands.

It took the paramedics forty-five minutes to arrive but it takes them under five minutes to leave. Two of them move Zulma to the stretcher after a minor struggle with the headset, cover her with a white sheet and take her away. One minute here, fifty minutes later you're gone — the usual platitudes are exchanged in the kitchen. Eventually they all go back to their terminals and resume their work.

The first call Juli takes is from an old man complaining that he can hear people talking in the background when he's on the line. Here they are now, he says, and asks Juli whether she can hear them. Juli — who can't hear anything out of the ordinary — asks if it couldn't actually be his neighbours who are talking, but the man is adamant the voices are on the line, not in his flat, nor in his head, and that someone is using his phone without his permission. The conversation goes on for five minutes. Juli tries to reason with the man and hopes he'll lash out but he doesn't, and he just repeats the same couple of lines over and over politely. In the end he hangs up. Juli is left feeling empty, for the seven seconds it takes for the next call to come in.

A FOREIGN COUNTRY IS THE PAST

Then she works for three more hours, all easy calls. At the end of the shift, her average is one hundred and fifty seconds.

Before heading out, Juli lingers for a moment in front of Zulma's cubicle. Zulma's thick bottle-bottom glasses are resting on the desk, next to her red lipstick, some coins, a crumpled pack of national cigarettes, a latex glove left behind by the paramedics, and some unrecognisable food leftovers.

And the holy cards are still stapled to the cubicle wall. She can recognise Saint Francis — because of the funny hair — and Saint Cajetan — because of the wheat. There's one who's holding a massive staff, and another one with his body all pierced with arrows. There's one dressed like a Roman legionary (with a halo), and another one contorted and staring up at heaven. Another saint is praying in front of a crucifix. Another one has wings. Jesus is also there, nailed to the cross, because where else would he be? There are also photos of people who seem to be family members. Here she realises that she never talked about much with Zulma, that when they coincided in the kitchen during a break, their conversations were about work and the call centre — about what this or that customer had said, what this or that operator had done, their average times the previous day, Juli's contract nearing its end, not knowing if it'll be renewed, who'd got the sack the previous month, and so on. Maybe it was a self-defence mechanism, a way to shield their lives from the call centre. Either that, or they weren't really interested in one another.

The computer is still on and the file of the difficult customer is still open on the screen. Juli presses the power button and the computer sighs and shuts down. She leaves.

When she comes in the next day, Zulma's cubicle has been cleared. Gone are all her things — all the saints and the family photos, her glasses, the glove, the leftovers. It's as if Zulma had never existed. When Juli's cubicle is emptied next week, it'll look just like this. You wouldn't be able to tell one from the other — these twin cubicles in the large family of cubicles that is the call centre.

LOVE IS A CURABLE DISEASE

The words resonate somewhere in your head, spoken by your own voice, as if you were dictating them to yourself, for future preservation, or perhaps like a mantra. But you rarely talk to yourself, and never before felt the need to dictate yourself anything, or know what a mantra is, so the words take you by surprise. And for that reason, the words make such a strong impression. They are a revelation, given to you by who knows who. Love is a curable disease. Love is a curable disease. Love is a curable disease, your own voice says. And then you do the translation into a less poetic language: love is a waste of time. But how random, and how out of character, to have words in your head that don't deal with everyday minutiae, like "Do I need to refill the tank?" or "Where is the next service area?"

The words come to you while you are parking the car in this petrol station on a road in the middle of nowhere. Of course, you can't remember the name of this town, if there's even a town around, but you've been here before, several times, since it's on the way to the capital. There's the petrol station, and there's a decent grill at the back, cheap and full of truck drivers and other nomads, who are always up for a chat, who are always up to do the chatting, since you'd rather keep your cards to yourself, never give too much away, just snipe some phrases here and there for comedic effect. You know some of their names already, and they start to resemble something familiar — not friends nor a family, but no longer strangers. And then there's the girl who works at the till, love is a curable disease, who also plays the role of de facto waitress. She was here when you went south, was here when you returned, should be here again now. Very pretty girl, not the kind of girl you meet in petrol stations. Love might be a curable disease, but that doesn't mean you are dead.

You get out of the car, still with the words resonating in your head, feeling a bit uncomfortable about them by now. You walk to the trunk, open it, perhaps to confirm that the moccasins you've been selling from town to town for the past week are still there. Where would the shoes go? They have nowhere to go, and they need you to go places, and they need you more than you need them, because you could very well go from place to place peddling some other junk. But now that you think about it, it wasn't because of the shoes that you opened the trunk, but to get the deodorant from your bag, spray a bit under your armpits and crotch, because even if you are cured of love you don't want to walk into the grill smelling like a five-hour drive. Perhaps simply because you care about these things, and it's always nice to make the effort to be your best version of yourself. Especially because the girl at the till might be there today. Not that you are here because of her. It's just a coincidence that she works in the place where you need to stop, love is a curable disease.

Love is a curable disease. Yeah, well, whatever. They aren't even your words, they were a line from a song that played on the radio. But that you don't know, because you never pay attention to anything. So now they are your words. And now they are stuck in your head.

It's far from a dream job but it's regular. Something to make some easy cash until she figures out what to do with her life. Obviously no one bunks out of a Law degree in order to work at a petrol station. But she needed the mental space, and a job is a job as long as it pays. Sooner or later she'll figure out what to do, because things always make sense in the end.

Early start, early finish, only a couple of weekends a month, no nights because they only allow guys to do the night shift — because the truckies can't be trusted around young women, that's what the manager said. The money isn't great, but it doesn't even need to pay her much, as she doesn't have to pay rent any more, not for a while. And it's a straightforward job most of the time, and she can do plenty of reading, or just think. Time drags slowly in this job. And sometimes that's all you really need.

And to be absolutely fair, the mostly male clientele are OK. And if they aren't OK when they turn up, they are generally OK after some food and wine. They pay without ever checking the bill, which compensates for the lack of tips, since she can add a couple of digits here and there. Then they head to the parking lot to sleep off the wine.

And then they drive away, still pickled above the legal limit, but no one checks that kind of thing, not round here. And perhaps they return a month or so later, when the job brings them to this neck of the woods, and they walk into the station and head to the back to eat their greasy steaks, and meet a couple of old friends from the road. In a way, it's like a public service — helping people get together and have a good time.

And not just truckies. Because occasionally there are buses packed with school kids stopping for a toilet break on the way to the capital. And the random guys who look like travelling salesmen. And some other unexpected characters, which means the job can be interesting too. Yesterday, four nuns in a pick-up truck stopped for coffee — one of them was wearing the national football jersey, with "JESUS #1" written on the back. Last month, it was workers from a circus — one was dressed as a clown, make-up and all. Where the hell do these people live? In convents and circuses, is the right answer, but you don't get to see so many convents and circuses any more.

Entertaining or not, what sold her the job was not having to use her brain too much. That, and the convenience of living nearby, even if it means being back with her parents. Temporarily; only temporarily. An easy job, and when the day is done, she can jump on her bike and cycle just a few miles back home. And because there's nothing at all to do in town, she goes to bed early. It's like being on a retreat. All the mind power that she needs, for whatever it is she needs it.

A FOREIGN COUNTRY IS THE PAST

So now that you are all perfumed up, you walk into the petrol station bar. The pretty girl is there, behind the counter as you had anticipated, her young face semi-hidden behind cigarette brands. You walk towards her, your aviators still on, your shirt unbuttoned, your hairy chest visible, too visible. She waits for you with a faint smile on her face and you walk towards her slowly, exuding the comfort and security of someone who knows he's in control.

"Hello. What can I get you sir?" she asks.

"Hello... But don't call me, sir... I'm not that old!" you say.

"What can I get you?"

"Ezequiel's the name. But you can call me Eze," you say.

"What can I get you, sir?" she insists.

"Camel twenties, lights," you say. She grabs the Camels from the display, places them on the counter. You get your wallet out, grab a couple of notes, pay and wait for the change. "Serving food already?"

"Yes, we are. Grab a seat at the back and I'll take your order in a couple of minutes."

"And what should I call you?"

"You don't need to call me. I'll come over in a minute."

"Don't you have a name?" you say. Then you see the CELIA fluorescing by the price of the Camels on the till. "Celia must be someone else, then..."

"No, that's me."

"OK, Celia, see you in a bit," you say, and walk into the dining area. And you've already forgotten that love is a curable disease.

Wow, what a creepy old man. At least the truck drivers are blunt, and because they are so blunt they are a bit comical. These guys — the ones driving cars — are full of themselves, and you never know what weird nonsense they'll come up with.

Celia watches you on the CCTV screen, as you walk towards the back, nod to a bunch of guys in the corner, walk to the table with the big fat truck driver who arrived half an hour earlier. She sees you shake hands with him and then drop on the white plastic chair.

"How've you been, Rudolf Valentino? Long time no see!" says Moyano. He's sprawled all over the chair, his shirt slightly forced upwards by the pressure of his own stomach, the button that holds it closed about to shoot into the air.

"In the struggle, Moyano... Always in the struggle."

"Been doing time or something?"

"I've been on the seaside for a while. You know, to bank on the holidays. You have to follow the money, right?"

"Still selling those shirts? I need a new shirt."

"I can see that," you say. "I'm not doing textiles. I'm in footwear right now."

"I need a pair of new shoes too," Moyano says.

"I'll let you have a look at the shoes later. I've got some fantastic leather moccasins. Just like these ones," you say, and model them without standing up.

"Are they Italian?"

"No, a national brand. Way better than the Italians. Our leather is much better anyway."

"Is it real leather?"

"You could salt them, throw them on the grill right now, and eat them in ten minutes. That's how real the leather is."

"You sound hungry," says Moyano.

"Have you eaten yet?"

"Yes. The flank steak is just about right today. But avoid the black pudding."

"Well, I'll order some flank steak then… If that girl ever drops by."

"She must be intimidated by all that hair, Valentino," says Moyano.

And here you click your fingers and say "Celia!" a couple of times, until Celia comes out from behind the counter and walks to you with a notepad and a pen.

"Do you happen to have a bad memory or you want to take down my phone number?" you ask.

"I have a good memory but I need to pass the order to the grill master, don't I?" Moyano chuckles while you take her in from behind your aviators. "My colleague says the flank steak is quite good today… Is that right?"

"I can ask the grill master for a recommendation, sir," Celia says.

"No, Celia: I want your recommendation. And it's Ezequiel. Or just Eze. But not sir," you say.

"I don't eat meat," says Celia.

"Is it too expensive for you?"

"No. I just don't like it."

"Because if it's too expensive, I'd happily pay for a meal for you."

"That's very kind, sir, but it isn't necessary. So what can I get you then?"

"Are you in a rush?"

"I actually am," she says.

"I see it's really busy down here," you say and look around, as if you needed to confirm that it isn't.

"Yes. I've got lots of things to do," she says.

"Get me the flank steak, then. And a tomato and lettuce salad."

"And to drink?"

"Whatever my colleague is having."

"So a flank steak, a tomato and lettuce salad, and a jug of house wine."

"That's correct. Excellent memory," you say, and Moyano chuckles once more. Celia walks out of the room and into the kitchen. When she walks out both of you follow her bottom until it disappears past the door. The words "love is a curable disease" come to your head once more.

A while later, you are sinking your moustache in a glass of red wine. Of course, you don't know that Celia has spat in the jug. Maybe if you did, you'd still drink — because it'd be a way of being closer to her, of taking part in that intimate, timeless ritual of exchanging fluids. And later still, you are cutting a piece of flank steak, watching the blood paint the white plate red. Celia hasn't spat on the flank steak, but the meat tastes as good as if she had.

"So, how's the family?" asks Moyano, ambushing you.

"The family is good," you say, in between swallowing two bites.

A FOREIGN COUNTRY IS THE PAST

"You've got kids, right?"

"Yeah, two boys, seven and ten."

"Get to see them much?"

"When I can. They live with their mother."

"I see… So you split?"

"Yeah, you could say that."

"Hard to stay together in our line of work, right?"

"Guess so."

"You, younger lot, have it even harder than us. In my time you'd just hang on. Now everyone breaks up."

"Maybe," you say.

"You all just get a divorce and screw trying to make things work."

"It's quite common, yes."

"I'm going home this coming weekend."

"Which one of the homes?" you ask, and Moyano lets out a quiet laugh.

"The official one," he says and gets up from his chair, dangerously aiming his shirt button right at your face. "Be back soon," he says and heads towards the toilets in the back.

You stay with your food, relieved that you can eat in silence at least for a minute or two. But now you've lost your appetite. There are conversations that make you lose your appetite, even if love is a curable disease.

She feels guilty — she shouldn't have spat in the wine. But you made her feel something worse than guilt, and the guilt put that feeling to rest; so at least there's that. It's hard to say exactly what made her so uncomfortable. There's the pathetic flirting. And there's the way you treat her — as if you were above her, as if you were better and in control. But it's none of that either.

Celia gazes at the CCTV and sees you chewing in silence at the back. You are hunched over the table, sitting alone in one of those horrible plastic chairs. She can see the tucked-in shirt, the blue jeans. She can see that you aren't wearing socks — your hairy and vulnerable white ankles show above your moccasins. Who wears moccasins without socks but policemen? But you aren't a policeman. You don't even enjoy the authority that a gun and a uniform provide, and maybe for that reason, people spit in your wine.

The sight of your white ankles and your sockless moccasins make her feel sad for you. So that was it: sadness. Now she feels double guilty, because she spat in your wine, just because you made her feel sad. And feeling double guilty makes her feel angry. And she dislikes you even more. It's complicated. Things are always complicated. And that's why sometimes you need to quit your studies, take a job in a petrol station, take time to figure things out. Sometimes you just have to make time stop, lest you end up wearing moccasins without socks.

Some minutes later, Moyano joins you at the table once more.

"Is the coffee any good here?" he asks.

"Hopefully it's better than the flank steak," you say.

"What happened? Are you on a diet?" asks Moyano.

"I was hungry but this is like eating chewing gum with veins," you say.

A FOREIGN COUNTRY IS THE PAST

"Well, I don't know any Firestone Star restaurant round here..." says Moyano. "Do you?"

"Michelin," you say.

"Whatever," he replies.

By now the wine has got to your head and you can feel the tiredness of many kilometres weighing down on you. A coffee would be good, but there's still wine in the jug, and there's still time to drink it. And there's the thirst — there's always the thirst after a salty piece of meat. Or maybe it's the thirst of the road, and of those moccasins in the trunk, their dry leather sucking the humidity out of the world. You pull yourself another glass, Moyano does the same. Both ate the salty beef. Both are on the road. Both are thirsty.

"When are you showing me those shoes?" he asks.

"I was thinking about that. Want to go and take a look at them now?" you say. "I need to stretch my legs."

"Sure," says Moyano, and you head out taking your glasses with you.

When you walk past Celia you wink at her and she gifts you a forced smile. It doesn't matter if it's forced — it's still a smile. Moyano spots her and elbows you and you both laugh. And love is a curable disease. Love is a curable disease, once more, and you wish you could explain it to Moyano, but he wouldn't understand.

Soon you are opening the trunk with one hand. Then you unzip the large suitcase, trying to keep the liquid in the glass, partially succeeding. And there they are, the moccasins. You finish your wine in one gulp, toss the glass to the side — it falls on the grass and it doesn't break.

"Right, fatso. What size?"

"Forty-three," says Moyano.

"OK. Forty-three I've got both in brown and black."

"What do you reckon?"

"I'd say black. Black's more versatile. Brown's just casual. Not that anyone will see your shoes while you are stuck in that stinky truck," you say, and pull a bag of black moccasins, then another one, and then another one — this one size forty-three, black. "Try them on. If you get them, I can assemble a box for you."

Moyano sits on the trunk and the car lowers several centimetres. He takes his indescribable old shoes off. Now he's standing barefoot in the parking lot, stepping on his shoes to avoid the hot concrete. And here you spot his overgrown toenails, and feel better about yourself, because you'd never let yourself go like that. Moyano tries the right shoe first, then the left one. He stares at the moccasins as if he were staring at a riddle.

"Feel free to walk in them a bit," you say. "You need to walk in them to see how comfortable they are," you add, with your outstanding salesman's skills. He walks, awkwardly, back and forth.

"They feel comfortable, yes."

"Told you so, didn't I?"

"Will they be good for driving?"

"They'll be good for everything! Want to play football in them? They'd be good too. They are excellent shoes, I'm telling you. Just make sure they aren't too tight or too loose."

"They feel just right."

"Then they are right."

"How much are they?"

"They sell for one hundred wholesale, but for you, I'll leave them at seventy. Seventy and coffee."

"Deal," says Moyano. He takes the wallet from his back pocket, and gives you a few crumpled notes. You put the notes in your right pocket, zip back the suitcase, close the trunk.

"Shit, I forgot the box. Let me get you a box," you say, and start opening the trunk again.

"Don't worry about it," says Moyano. "I'll wear them."

"Coffee then," you say, and the two of you head back to the dining room, leaving Moyano's old shoes behind like abandoned snake skin.

Celia watches you walk past as you head to your table. Then she follows you on the screen as you take your seat. She can see you tidying up your shirt, so that it shows the right amount of chest. She walks towards you, notepad in hand.

"You won't need that, Celia," you say.

"What can I get you?"

"Your eternal love," you say — love is a curable disease, you think.

"I'm afraid we don't serve that," she says. Moyano laughs and you feel like he's laughing at you. And perhaps he is.

"Well, in that case, two black coffees. Put them on this distinguished gentleman's bill," you say and Moyano nods, smiling proud in his new moccasins. She nods and walks away.

"She loves me," you say.

"Not sure about that, Valentino," says Moyano.

"She's just playing hard to get."

"Maybe she doesn't like you, Valentino," he says, and you know he's right but you still won't admit it.

"If you give up at the first hurdle, you'll never get anywhere," you say, and watch Celia come back to the table, carrying two cups of coffee. You follow her in silence, resentful because you can't risk another clever comeback with Moyano here. "Thanks," you say and then watch her walk away in silence.

You have a sip of coffee and burn your tongue. "The coffee is worse than the meat," you say.

Moyano gives a half-hearted shrug. And love is a curable disease.

"So… I better get going," you say, standing up.

"Heading out so soon?" he asks.

"Those shoes don't shift themselves. When are you heading out?"

"I'll take a nap at the back of the truck, and then make a move. Can't be driving after all that wine."

"A wimp, that's what you are! Where are you heading to?"

"First home for the weekend."

"Ah, yes."

"Then I've got some short back-and-forth jobs. And then back round here for a few weeks."

"Might catch you then."

"You might. See if you can get me a nice couple of shirts."

A FOREIGN COUNTRY IS THE PAST

"I still need to shift hundreds of shoes, but I might move back to textiles soon. I'll keep you posted — that shirt you're wearing is twenty kilos too old," you say and you both laugh. You shake hands with him and head to the till to settle the bill. Celia is already waiting with it on the counter.

"There you go," you say. "Keep the change."

"Thanks," she says, too polite to tell you to shove those two miserable coins up your arse.

"Can I borrow your pen for a second?" you ask.

"Sure," says Celia and extends a biro. You grab it, write your name and telephone number on the bill, fold it, pass it back to Celia.

"If you ever fancy a coffee somewhere else, give me a call," you say, pointing at the bulky mobile phone hanging from your belt. "I'm often round here."

"OK," says Celia.

"OK," you say and walk out, glancing back at her every now and then.

So sad, she thinks, as she tosses the paper in the bin. Before you start the engine, she has already forgotten your name. She doesn't even watch as you drive erratically out of the parking lot.

Fields as far as the eye can see. The land that never ends. And the road is just a straight line cutting across the fields, not a curve in sight. No other cars in either direction. Just your car shooting fast on the road, leaving trees and trees behind, and other trees appear, and love is still a curable disease, but screw that, since you can drive away from it all, and you better play some music to keep you awake. But there are no radios around here in the middle of nowhere.

Fata morgana, always a couple of hundred metres away, always winning the race. The sun dancing on the road, then the sun in your eyes. Every now and then, your eyelids come close to meeting but you keep going, with the sun in your eyes, been going for too long and you can't give up now — this isn't the moment to fall asleep. The temptation to let go is strong but there's Celia, and she will call you; you just know she will call you one day, because love is a curable disease, but some still end up terminally ill, can't get away from love, can't drive away from it, and you might be one of them, the ones who can't stop loving, or at least searching for love, or something that you often confuse with love, and she might be one of them too. The life that you could start together, the way her skin smells in the morning, her dresses on her side of the wardrobe, her body lotions and creams in the bathroom cabinet, the way they take up most of the space, but it's fine like that, it's fine. Then there's the moccasins in the trunk — you need to shift those moccasins, find something else to sell, something more interesting, something that doesn't suck the humidity out of the world, you don't know, encyclopaedias, Tupperware, imported gadgets, whatever. You nod off and it could have been a split second or a few hours that your eyelids spent together, and then you pull your head back against the headrest, and you keep going like there's no tomorrow, even if you have nowhere to get to; your right foot pressing the pedal, your right black leather moccasin pressing the gas pedal, and the moccasins in the trunk sucking the humidity out of the world, and the trees keep scrolling to the sides, and the land that never ends, and the fata morgana, and another nod, and one more, your head against the headrest, and the trees, the fata morgana, Celia's smile, the fields that never end, the way she smells, her dresses in the wardrobe, the moccasins, the way her mouth smells in the morning, her creams in the cabinet, another nod, and Celia's beautiful smile, so full of love, a birthday cake, and her eyes that shine when she stares at you, her eyes that shine when they lock on yours and she says "Eze, I love you."

But before the black screen, the moccasins. Can you believe it? The moccasins. Of all the things in the world, the moccasins.

The right foot pushes the right pedal, then the left foot pushes the left pedal, and so on, that's how bicycles work, no need to invent the wheel, when the wheel is already invented and there are two of them, one following the other in a straight line, moving on the cracked dirt road.

Celia cycles on the side road that leads back to town, the road that runs parallel to the highway, the service road with the fields, some weekend houses, and just about that for several kilometres. It's already cool enough for the ride to be pleasant, and the smell of wet wheat, and the land that never ends on one side, and the trees that she leaves behind, and the ones that come at her, both sides of the dirt road, no fata morgana on a dirt road. It won't take her long to get home. It won't take her an eternity — just fifteen, twenty minutes at most.

The air is cool and perfumed this time of the day, and she wishes the ride would take longer. Because when she gets home, there'll be nothing to do but listen to her parents' silence — their silent disappointment — as they drink *mate* in the garden, and wait for the time to sit in silence in front of the telly. They don't understand. They will never understand that she needed time to stop for a while. She doesn't even understand herself. She just knows that's what she needed.

And she pushes one pedal, and then the other pedal, and on she goes, unbothered by the sounds of sirens on the highway a kilometre west, two more screaming fire trucks darting off to rescue whatever they can from the car that half an hour or so earlier crashed headfirst against a truck parked on the hard shoulder. When they get there and join the other firefighters they'll find mostly torn iron, hundreds of shoes scattered all over the road, all brown or black, many in flames, masking the smell of burning human flesh. They'll have to cut the car open to rescue whatever is left inside — whatever the fire hasn't already burnt to a cinder.

But all of this Celia will never know, because she'll turn right soon, taking the road by the cemetery, where old white mausoleums loom over the walls. And now the birds have muffled the sirens, and maybe that's the cue to pedal slower. Maybe she just needs to pedal slowly, listen to the birds for a bit longer. Or perhaps she just needs to stop, and sit on a tomb for a while. For what's the rush now? What's the rush now that time passes so slowly?

ASHES

"Today we're taking my Grandpa and Grandma for a car ride."

Paula doesn't reply and keeps staring at her mobile phone. Mother doesn't reply either, and stays hypnotised by her show. It's one of those morning TV hells where presenters tear people apart for a roaring audience. While a sobbing peroxide blonde talks about sleeping with her brother-in-law, I sneak into the lounge, and soon I'm in the shed forcing Grandma's urn open with the peen of a rusty hammer. It's already quite hot and I'm sweating before I begin, but at least the top surrenders at the first attempt. Inside there's a small transparent bag. I pull it out and look in: ashes and tiny bone fragments; it must weigh a couple of hundred grams, no more than that. Next I do Grandpa's and it's the same — they say couples end up looking like one another in time, and I guess they're right. I remove the little ID plaques and pocket them. Then I return the ashes to the urns, loosely replace the covers, and stash my grandparents one on top of the other in a supermarket bag.

The supermarket must have opened since I was last here nine years ago — I don't recognise its name.

It happened fast.

His right leg started to turn black around early spring, and before summer they chopped it off. A couple of months later, he was legless and mindless. But it was Grandma who kicked the bucket first, out of nowhere. Friday afternoon she was watering the hydrangeas; Saturday morning the strong stomach pains started, and mother called an ambulance and Grandma was driven straight to A&E.

I was there when she died a week later. I arrived at the prearranged time, to find a doctor and Mother waiting outside the intensive care unit. The doctor asked if I really wanted to see her, said that she was dying, that I had to properly understand what was going on, because this wasn't the kind of stuff people should do without proper understanding. I said that I understood and went in. Grandma was wearing a mask, and there were pipes and cables and machines with lights and beeping sounds. She was conscious and held my hand and like that she passed away.

One minute here and the next minute gone.

It's quite strange, if you think about it. I'm not sure there's anything to understand. I'm not sure it can be understood.

And now she's in a supermarket bag, with Grandpa on top — very likely for the first time in half a century.

The supermarket has a foreign name. Mother says that most supermarkets in town are now Chinese, that everyone now says "I'm going to the Chinese" when they mean "I'm going to the supermarket." But then everyone here is racist. I wasn't aware that everyone here is racist when I left exactly twenty years ago today. April 13, 2002: exactly twenty years ago. I hadn't realised this either. I'm not sure why I clock it right now, when Mother tells me about the Chinese supermarket.

And, of course, I hadn't planned to deal with the ashes today because of an anniversary that I ignored. I just happened to be back home today, and Mother finally gave up, after I'd banged on for years that she couldn't keep the ashes among her books forever. But there's a certain ring to the number twenty, something round, and now I can't see how I could possibly deal with the ashes any other day.

A few months after Grandma's death, Grandpa was sent to a residential home. He soon took to painting, shit painting — not as in bad quality painting, but as in a *dirty protest*. Apparently he'd stick his index finger under the nappies, scoop some shit out, and design abstractions on the wall next to the bed. The residential home manager called one afternoon to tell me about it. I borrowed Mother's car and drove there with some cash to keep the manager happy, and to interview the artist.

Grandpa didn't acknowledge his creative feats, said that he had never painted with shit. Then he spent the rest of my visit talking about the porn films the nursing staff would shoot at night, using some of the vacant beds in the room. The description of the filming gear was quite convincing, but the scenes didn't seem to match the sexual mores of the time.

And now he's also in a Chinese supermarket bag, as I drive on the riverside avenue. I'm driving them both, Grandma and Grandpa, unbelted on the passenger seat. And I'm driving Mother and Paula too, sitting in the back, their belts securely fastened.

Everything has changed around here, and I can't find a spot to access the river. There's the sand processing plant where Grandpa and I used to go fishing, but now there's a sentry box with a security guard at the entrance. And there's the marina by the park, but that's where the sewers discharge, and even if Grandma once said she wanted her ashes flushed down the toilet, that was over twenty years ago, and she might have changed her mind since then. And then there's Paula, and things need to be handled sensitively, lest she take a terrible memory of this place back to London.

"Where are we going, Dad?" she asks.

"We're taking my Grandparents for a ride," I say, recycling my joke.

"But where?" she asks.

"I've got no idea, no idea, just enjoy the ride... By the way, that's where I used to play every day when I was your age," I say, pointing with my head towards the park. It looks much smaller than I remembered it; the grass is dry and the kids kicking a football raise dust clouds.

Grandpa croaked alone. I'd spent some hours with him during the day, in the hospital room where they'd taken him when he started with the chest pains. They didn't let me stay the night. When the phone rang at precisely three in the morning, I knew exactly what'd happened — you always know someone's dead when the phone rings at three in the morning.

We drove with mother to the hospital. He was lying on a stretcher, covered with a blanket I didn't lift. I can't remember much more, only that I was relieved he'd died. Because it put an end to his decay, but also because I had a plane to catch four days later — not a holiday but an exit plan. Would I have left all the same if he hadn't died? Pointless to ask that question now.

That was twenty years and four days ago. There was no shit painting in that hospital room. Not on the walls.

I drive to the old pier and park the car nearby. The entrance is now boarded up. Mother says that they must have shut it off when a large section of the pier fell into the river seven years ago. I get out to look for a way to sneak in, but the fence is too high and there's barbed wire everywhere. I go back to the car and soon we're heading north. Mother says that most of the beaches are now boarded up too, that the city sold them to build tower blocks and gated communities on the waterfront. We might end up flushing the ashes down the toilet after all.

But I keep driving along the riverside avenue, towards the docks where the passenger ships leave for the islands. It's midweek and low season, and we might find a quiet spot to scatter the ashes.

The old riverside promenade looks more or less the same — just a few more bars on the beach. The rowing club is still there, and they've painted the ridiculously English clubhouse blue. The fishermen's quarter is still standing; the shops are now closed, but the fishermen will soon return on their boats and hang their haul out to die in the sun.

"I'm hungry," says Paula, never lifting her eyes from her mobile phone.

"As soon as we're done with this, we'll grab something to eat. You can eat very fresh fish round here."

"But I don't like fish," she says.

"And what would you like to eat?"

"I don't know."

"Maybe we can order Chinese," I say.

"I don't like Chinese either," she says.

Mother nods along.

I can't remember if it was when Grandma or Grandpa died, because both funerals were held in the same directors', and in my mind they blur together. Uncle and I were drinking coffee at the petrol station in the corner, taking a break from the rest of the family and the stench of flowers. He was there throughout the whole thing, both times, because mother was broken and useless, and there were still things I needed to figure out about the admin of other people's deaths.

I can't remember what we talked about with Uncle either, only that he was there. He was a simple but nice man, and this is a good memory. It takes me away from all the sorrow, even if we were drinking coffee during a funeral. Mother says he was terrified when it was his turn, that he behaved like a child, crying all the way into nothingness. But who are the living to judge?

I don't know where they held his funeral, nor what happened to his ashes, if he was cremated. I was already away when he died, and people don't wait for you to return when it's their time to go.

I park the car in the empty parking lot by the docks. There are two guys fishing on the northern end of the elevated esplanade, but the other side is deserted. I can see some stairs leading to the beach there.

I feel like a criminal, carrying my Chinese supermarket bag — there's always something criminal in the disposing of a body. Two bodies. Ashes. But it has to be done, had to be done for a long time. The thought of them on that shelf has haunted me for twenty years.

Some weeks ago, still in London, I had a dream. I was in Mother's house and there was a weird green slimy matter dripping from the ceiling and leaking from under the skirting. The slime flowed and flowed, and I couldn't make it stop. It smelled of hydrangeas and cigarettes. I woke up sweating and decided right then that the ashes wouldn't stay in that house after this trip.

I can see her watering her flowers in her light blue summer dress. I can see him smoking in the corner, leaning against a lamppost.

Then I can't see them any more.

We go down the stairs. The beach is fine here: sand, no rubbish, there's a short wooden jetty opening into the river. The men fishing on the other end of the esplanade can't see us, and there's no one rowing or swimming right now. No boats, no yachts, no ships, no kayaks, nothing but the river and the islands, beautiful across the water. I get the urns out of the Chinese supermarket bag, place them on a wooden plank, and remove the covers. The ashes, in their little nylon bags, get some sun for the first time in twenty years — they shine. I watch Paula draw two hearts in the sand with a stick. I feel Mother's presence behind me, but I don't want to turn around and meet her eye.

Now I just need to scatter the ashes — that's all I need to do. Get the little bags out of the urns, and just scatter the ashes, let the river take them away. And then we'll grab something to eat. And then we'll get on with our lives.

Scattering these ashes is all I need to do right now. It's the simplest thing in the world.

ABOUT THESE STORIES

Of these fifteen stories, only three were previously published in different versions: 'Sunstroke', 'Pier', and 'Ashes', all of which appeared in *The London Magazine* between 2021 and 2023. 'Pier' won the London Magazine Short Story Prize in 2021.

ABOUT THE AUTHOR

Fernando Sdrigotti is the author of several books and pamphlets, including *Shitstorm* (Open Pen, 2018), *Jolts* (Influx Press, 2020), and *We Are But Nothing* (Rough Trade Books, 2023). Born in Argentina in the mid-70s, he has lived in London since the early 2000s.

Influx Press is an independent publisher based in London, committed to publishing innovative and challenging literature from across the UK and beyond.

www.influxpress.com
@Influxpress

THANKS TO OUR KICKSTARTER SUPPORTERS

Eva Aldea
Jennifer Bernstein
Polly Chapman
Anne Charnock
Matthew Colbeck
Amanda Dackombe
Marianna Datsenko
Bill Godber
Rob Jackson
Neil D.A. Stewart
Carsten ten Brink
Goutham Veeramachaneni
Teresa Young

THANKS TO OUR LIFETIME SUPPORTERS

D. Franklin
Barbara Richards
Bob West